BLACK OUT

D1559580

BIEN-AIME WENDA

· B L A C K · O U T ·

To
the
earth angels

• B L A C K • O U T •

PROLOGUE

It all began like the arrival of a California earthquake on a still autumn morning. No signs, no warnings, not even an omen. One minute thirteen-year-old Rusty Haynes Jr. was fast asleep in his parent's two-bedroom trailer, and the next minute, his ma was standing over him with a tattered straw broomstick. If that weren't strange enough, he was stunned to find his pa aiming a 1957 Remington rifle right at him. Both were still in their pajamas.

"What the hell are you doing in my boy's bed?" Rusty Sr. shouted.

Rusty Jr. crinkled his brows. "*Hunh?*"

Judy Haynes began swatting at the boy's head. "Where is he, *nigger?!*"

Rusty Jr.'s heart sped as he tried to block his mother's attacks. "What's goin' on?"

"I'll handle this." Rusty Sr. said to his wife.

He slowly took a step forward until the barrel of the Remington was pressed firmly against the boy's forehead. The sinister look in his blue eyes frightened his son.

"Listen here, nigger, you got 'xactly three seconds to tell me what you've done with Rusty, or I'm fixin' to put a hole right through that thick nigger skull of yours."

The boy's heart palpitated as he pleaded, "Pa! *It's me!*"

"What you call me?"

Rusty Sr. swung the butt of the rifle at the boy's head but wasn't fast enough. The boy grabbed the long barrel and pushed it against his father's stomach as they both began tussling for control of the gun.

"Pa! It's me!" The boy shouted, with tears clouding his eyes.

"Judy!" Rusty Sr. hollered. "Help me out here!"

Judy stood frozen behind them with both her hands covering her mouth. They were both moving about so quickly, she didn't know what to do.

She finally dashed out the bedroom, ran through their quaint living room, and into the kitchen to grab a large butcher knife. Just as she was making her way back to her son's bedroom, she heard a deafening blast throughout the small trailer.

"Russell?! Russ!!" Judy hollered.

Her flimsy blue house slippers ran to the bedroom and halted at the gruesome sight of her husband lying on the dull hardwood floor, with a pool of blood rushing from the side of his head.

The blood continued to spill out of the hole in his cranium, as she held his head onto her lap. "Rusty! Rustyyyyy!"

"Mama, I didn't mean to! Honest, I didn't!" Rusty Jr. sobbed. His hands trembled as he held on to the rifle.

Enraged, Judy Haynes grabbed the butcher knife from beside her and swiftly leapt to her feet to charge at the colored boy.

"Mama! No!" He cried out. Desperate, he aimed the rifle directly at the woman.

Unaffected by the threat of the gun, Judy Haynes attempted to plunge the butcher knife into his chest but missed.

She continued to flail the butcher knife wildly, while threatening to chop his limbs to pieces. Rusty tripped onto the ground, causing the gun to slip from his hand. He recoiled and braced himself for the brutal pain that he knew was sure to come with being butchered alive. That is, until he spotted the rifle at his side.

CHAPTER

ONE

Russell Haynes Jr. was born thirteen years ago to Russell Haynes Sr. and Judith Michelle Haynes. Mr. and Mrs.
Haynes had three children altogether: Nathaniel, Julia, and
Rusty Jr.. Their oldest, Nathaniel Haynes, had been killed
years ago during combat in Vietnam at the age of twenty.
Their only daughter, Julia Haynes, had run away to San
Francisco right after high school with Seymour Montgomery, a colored boy. Both Rusty Sr. and Judy Haynes disowned
their daughter after discovering she had married Seymour
and given birth to their only granddaughter, Jordyn Rose
Montgomery, whom they also disowned. News travelled fast
in Saint Molasses, and for years the Haynes would become
the topic of all gossip amongst men and women, coloreds and
whites alike. Negroes and whites running off together was
not only unheard of, but frowned upon in Saint Molasses.

The small Mississippi town of Saint Molasses had a pop-
ulation of barely 800. In fact, the town was so small, there
was only one library, one school, one pharmacy, and one ma-
jor grocery store. If one wished to visit a museum, shopping
mall, night club, or movie theater, they'd have to travel a couple miles over to the city of Marmalade to do so.

Like most small rural towns, everybody knew everybody.
Depending on what you were up to, that could either be a

good thing or a bad thing. For instance, if you had a passion for chasing skirts, like Sonny O'Donnell, then it was probably a bad thing. Just ask Mrs. O'Donnell, who demanded her husband take his "whores" to the inn over in Marmalade if he insisted on cheating. She'd grown tired of being a recurring topic of the town's gossip. That's the type of thing that came with being a resident of a small town. Everyone knew everyone. Which would explain why Frederick, a visitor, had been receiving odd looks ever since his Plymouth Fury had overheated, right in front of the town's welcome sign.

It had taken almost an entire day for nineteen-year-old Frederick King to find an auto shop that would fix his automobile. Every mechanic he'd brought his vehicle to had either outright told him they didn't service coloreds or had given him a quote of an astronomical figure. He finally ran into a townsman at a local drug store who was willing to point him in the right direction, but by that time, night was slowly creeping in.

"There's a mechanic shop, Lucky Man's Auto & Repair." The white gentleman said, whose hair reminded Frederick of Elvis Presley. He pointed east, then said, "Just head down that road and make the first left. Can't miss it."

"Thanks a lot, sir." Frederick said. Heading towards his car, he heard the man mumble something. "You say somethin'?"

"I said," The man began, drawing near. "I said, it's almost seven. Everything's fixin' to close in a few minutes."

"Y'all got any motels around here?"

"Next town over." The man answered.

"How far is that?"

"'Bout a few miles."

Frederick glanced back at his Plymouth. "Think she'll make it?"

The man looked at the ten-year-old car. "Can't say. Where ya' from?" The man asked, curiously eyeing the younger man's Timberland boots, baggy jeans, and black fitted cap with a giant white X printed across it.

"Negus."

"Negus." The man repeated. "I reckon it's been a helluva lot of years since I been outta Saint Molasses. Don't think I can say I ever heard of it."

"You wouldn't have heard of it." Freddie informed.

The man furrowed his brows. "I don't catch ya' drift."

"Thanks for ya help, sir." He said, ignoring the confusion on the man's face. "You were the only person willing to help a brother out. Appreciate that."

The man's cheek's flushed with embarrassment. "I wouldn't call it helping."

"*Hey.*" Margaret Browne, one of the oldest residents in town, called out. A round white woman with sky blue hair, the widow was known as the town's busiest busybody. She squinted in their direction before asking, "Everything alright?"

The white man lifted a hand. "Everything's alright, Mrs. Browne."

"I don't mind going back in to have Albert phone the sheriff." She offered, pointing at the drug store.

"It's alright, Mrs. Browne." He repeated more firmly. He turned his attention back to the young man. "You'd best hurry along and go on to the next town if I were you. Quickly."

Freddie nodded. "You're not from around here yourself, are you?" Freddie asked.

The man peered into Freddie's eyes suspiciously. He blinked when he thought he'd seen the iris of the boy's eyes flicker blue. "Originally from Dayton. Dayton, Ohio. Is it that obvious?" He smiled.

Freddie pressed his lips together as he smiled back. "Thanks for your generosity, sir. I gotta get going." He said. He was about to turn towards his vehicle when he halted, as if suddenly remembering something. "Don't you forget where you came from, Jimmy. Don't ever forget."

Before he could ask how he'd known his name, the young man, and his Plymouth Fury vanished into thin air.

Bug-eyed, Jimmy turned to face Margaret. "Did ya' see-" His voice trailed off as he watched the elderly woman's body go limp. With her dark brown eyes still stretched open in shock, he rushed to her side before her body could hit the concrete.

CHAPTER

TWO

"*P*olice *are asking anyone who may have any information on the brutal slaying of Russell Haynes Senior and Judith Haynes, as well as the disappearance of their thirteen-year-old son, Russell Haynes Jr., to please contact the sheriff's office at....*" The news anchor spouted off the number as a photo of a smiling Rusty Jr. with bright red hair was shown on screen.

"Isn't it just horrible?" Georgia Daniels asked, cupping a slender hand over her red painted lips. "We shouldn't have to hear about this on the day of Judy Garland's death. I'm depressed enough as it is."

Jimmy squinted at the black-and-white television in their living room. "Russell and Judith Haynes? Isn't that-"

Georgia's full blonde ringlets bounced as she interrupted, "Don't you remember? Mr. Haynes is the short fella with the red hair who works at that janky ol' car lot."

Jimmy eyes lit up in recognition as he nodded. "That's right. He tried to sell us that yellow Mustang for three times the price, when I specifically asked for the Thunderbird. Eyes lit up soon as you told him I was a lawyer. Con artist is what he is."

Georgia's eyes filled with fear as she shoved her husband. "The man is dead, Jimmy! And the killer is still out there somewhere."

"I'm sure they'll catch the bastard sooner than later. There's only so many places you can hide in this town."

Georgia scooted closer to him as she whispered, "They even killed his poor wife! It could've easily been me. I'm home alone all day while you're at work. The maid is only here for a coupla' hours every morning."

"Maybe you can hang out over at Eugenia's while I'm at work until the killer is caught. Hell, you could always pick up a part-time job so you're not at home alone during the day."

"A *job*? This isn't a joke, Jimmy." Georgia replied. "May the good Lord find Rusty Jr. Poor kid. Shoot, maybe I will drive over to Eugenia's during the day. Eugenia and Oliver just bought a nice big RCA color television set. It'd be downright groovy to watch Guiding Light in color."

Jimmy groaned, knowing that it was only a matter of time before Georgia would start pestering him to buy a color T.V.

"Told you we should've moved to Ohio." Georgia said.

Jimmy frowned. "You don't know anyone in Ohio. Why on earth would we move out there?"

"That's beside the point." She said. "You have family in Dayton. It's not like we would've been totally alone."

He shifted uneasily. "I told you, I haven't spoken to them in years. Besides, I'm sure you and Eugenia would miss each other if we moved."

Georgia held onto his arm. "You might have a point. Eugenia's like a sister to me." She sighed. "I don't know why they just don't run those people out of town." Georgia pouted.

"What people?"

Georgia scowled. "Those nig—those coloreds." She quickly corrected herself, remembering the fight she and her husband had gotten into the last time she had called their maid a nigger.

13

He gave her a quizzical look. "What have they ever done to you?" He asked. "Our housekeeper's colored for god sake."

She reared her head back as her blue eyes widened. "Who cares? They're *all* savages. Police said the killer was a darkie. We've done nothing but helped these people by providing them with jobs and education and whatnot, and this is how they repay us?"

Jimmy shook his head in disagreement. "They also said they had never seen a colored man with blue eyes in Saint Molasses before. It was confirmed that the killer was an outsider. It isn't any of the colored folks already living here, Georgia."

"They're all the same far as I'm concerned. They've all got the same jungle blood runnin' in 'em. This is the exact reason why I'm against integration." She spewed, crossing her arms. "Those animals just can't be tamed."

Jimmy shook his head in disdain.

"Only an animal would murder a helpless woman and child in cold blood, Jimmy."

"They didn't say the boy was murdered."

"Don't be so naïve. The boy is dead."

Jimmy pulled away from his wife and stood up from the sofa.

She looked up at him, suddenly afraid to be left alone. "Where yer goin'?"

Away from you, he wanted to say. "Jesus, can't a man take a leak without his wife givin' em the third degree?"

He walked off towards the bathroom, not waiting for a response from Georgia. Once inside, he immediately turned on the faucet and splashed the cold water on his face.

He stared at his reflection in the mirror. "Nah, it couldn't have been." He muttered to himself. "The boy they're lookin' for has blue eyes. He didn't have blue eyes. I'm almost sure of it." He didn't sound convincing even to himself. Had he imagined seeing the boy's eyes flicker blue? What if it was him? His wife was right. That could have easily been Georgia and himself murdered. He had almost invited the stranger to spend the night at their home, right before he just up and disappeared. Had he actually disappeared into thin air?

Don't you forget where you came from, Jimmy. Don't ever forget. What exactly had he meant by that?

CHAPTER

THREE

Dressed in blue blood-stained flannel pajamas, Rusty sneakers slammed against the pavement as he literally ran for his life. Hearing sirens in the distance, he had no doubt they were en route to his parents' trailer.

It all felt like a dream to Rusty, like an alternate reality. One minute his parents were...well, his parents. The next, they were trying to kill him as if they hadn't raised him the last thirteen and a half years.

Sniffling, he used a sleeve to wipe his wet blue eyes. Slowing down to catch his breath, he spotted his junior high school's vacant baseball field. He ran towards the stadium, figuring he could hide beneath the bleachers.

Fitting snugly underneath the seats, Rusty released a soft sputter that sounded like a cough. He squeezed his eyes shut and held his mouth open as he sobbed quietly. He couldn't wrap his head around the fact that he was now an orphan or the fact that it had been *him* who had murdered his parents. Other than hunting for racoons and rabbits with his pa, Rusty Jr. had never taken a life.

He looked down at the pigment of his hands. For the umpteenth time, he tried rubbing the top of his hand with the sleeve of his pajamas as hard as he could. Whatever this was on his skin, would not rub off.

"Good grief." He mumbled tearfully. The paint, or whatever it was, seemed to have set in deep.

Growing angrier by the second, Rusty scratched at his head in frustration. He leapt a few inches off the ground, bumping his head on the steel directly above him, at the feel of the coarse texture of his hair.

"What in tarnation?!" He cried, pulling at the puffy hair on his head. Yanking out a strand of hair, his eyes bucked at the sight of the tightly coiled dark red strand, instead of his own stringy bright red hair.

"Mama." He sobbed longingly. His tears seemed to be never-ending as they cascaded over his cheeks and onto his soiled pajamas.

"Somebody out here?"

Rusty stiffened at the deep baritone of a man's voice calling out from the outfield.

"Anybody out here?" A much friendlier voice echoed.

Rusty held his breath as two pairs of patent leather shoes trudged in the grass towards the bleachers. They stopped a few feet away from him.

"There's no one here." Deep voice said. "Told you to take Mrs. Abbott's word with a grain of salt."

The second man sighed. "Well she seemed pretty adamant that she seen a colored boy run this way."

"That old wench is pushing a 'hunnet, Bailey. Could've been staring at a smudge on her spectacles for all we know."

The second man was skeptical. "Gave a pretty accurate description, you ask me. Same description the neighbor 'cross the street from the Haynes gave."

"There ain't nobody here and frankly, I just wanna get home to Earline's meat loaf and sweet potato pie." Deep voice admitted impatiently.

The second man sighed. "Alright. I'll let the sheriff know."

Rusty waited until he could no longer hear or see the patent leather shoes of the two men, before he stopped holding his breath. Had it been any other day, he would have asked for help. He would've turned himself in and explained why he had done what he did. How it had been an act of self-defense. How it had all been a bizarre day. He would've told it all, from start to finish. However, as young as he was, even he knew it would be stupid to expect them to help him. Not in a colored body, anyway. If there was one thing Saint Molasses, Mississippi was known for, it was their hatred of outsiders and niggers.

CHAPTER
FOUR

"Sure it was a Plymouth?" Detective Dylan Ford's baritone voice probed.

"Positive." Margaret Browne answered, rearranging the dollies on her armchair, before taking a seat across from the two detectives. "Would you boys care for somethin' to drink?"

"No, thank you, ma'am." Detective Ford declined.

She looked at the other detective.

"No, thank you." Detective Edward Bailey replied. He looked down at his pocket-size notepad before proceeding. " Do you remember the color of the automobile, Mrs. Browne?"

Margaret squinted up at the ceiling as she stroked her chin. "I reckon it might've been red or brown. Maybe blue?"

Detective Ford threw his partner an exasperated glance. He had tried to tell Bailey before arriving at the old woman's two-story home, that getting reliable information from elderly residents had proven to be a waste of time.

"I know it was dark in color. I'm certain of it."

"And you're sure it was a nigger with blue eyes behind the wheel?" Ford questioned impatiently.

"No." Margaret scolded the detective. "I never said I seen him behind the wheel. He was outside the automobile when I seen him. I remember thinking that he looked like such a

19

stranger nigger, with his blue eyes and strange clothes and what-not."

"Strange clothes?" Detective Bailey repeated.

She nodded. "Yes. He weren't dressed like the other niggers that live over yonder on the southside. His pants were too big, so was his shirt. He wore a baseball cap turned the wrong way. Oh, and his shoes! They weren't Oxfords or-what's the other ones?"

"Keds?" Bailey asked.

"Keds. They weren't those. Very strange-looking, know what I mean? Very suspicious looking colored."

"Did he go in the Brooks Pharmacy at all, ma'am?' Ford asked.

She shook her head. "I don't think so. I only seen him outside for about a coupla' minutes 'fore his car just vanished into thin air." Margaret Browne, explained.

Bailey looked up from his notepad. "Vanished?"

"Yes, Ed. Vanished. I reckon it's the craziest thing I ever did see in my seventy-somethin' years of livin'. I'm telling you, this is a prophecy straight out of the book of Revelations." She looked at Detective Ford. "I haven't seen you and Moriah at service lately past coupla' Sundays. Everything alright at home, Dylan?"

Detective Ford sighed as he ignored the busybody's interrogation. "Mrs. Browne, I'm gonna leave my card with my direct number on it. Please don't hesitate to call if you remember something else about that night."

"I sure will." She replied, accepting the business card.

"You have a great one, Mrs. Browne." Bailey said, rising from the plastic-covered suede sofa.

"Oh wait, I just remembered somethin'." Margaret announced. "Someone else was out there when all this went down." She informed.

20

"Who's that?" Ford asked.

"Jimmy."

"Jimmy?" Bailey repeated, jotting the name.

Margaret nodded. "Yes. I forget his last name. Can't remember much these days."

Again, Detective Ford looked at Bailey. They had wasted enough time.

Bailey refused to meet Ford's gaze. "Jimmy Sterling? The hog farmer?" He asked the old woman.

"No. Not that Jimmy. You know, that sharp rich fella married to that gorgeous blonde? She looks just like one 'em movie stars and he looks just like Elvis Presley. Those two are another one I haven't seen at church in months."

Ford snapped his fingers as his eyes lit up. "You talkin' about Jimmy Daniels?"

"Jimmy Daniels. That's the name." She smiled. "It's a good thing he was there when he was. Almost cracked my skull wide open, had it not been for Jimmy."

"Can you tell us why you think we should speak to Jimmy Daniels?"

"Jimmy and the nigger were outside talking for some time before the nigger and his car just-*poof*-disappeared into thin air." She explained.

This time, Detective Bailey met his partner's doubtful gaze.

"The car did what-now?" Ford questioned.

Mrs. Browne nodded. "Might sound crazy, but it just up and vanished. Right 'fore my eyes."

21

CHAPTER

FIVE

Rusty waited for nightfall before trekking through his small town. On foot, Saint Molasses seemed much bigger to him. It was the first time he was grateful for the lack of city lights in Saint Molasses. He managed to find a half-eaten bear claw in the alley of the only Dixie Cream Donuts in town. He could have never in a million years imagine he would ever be so thankful to find a Dixie Cream cup filled with half-melted ice inside the dumpster. He spent the remainder of his night scrounging dumpsters in alleyways for anything he could salvage for later to eat.

Realizing that the following day would be a school day, Rusty decided that it was best not to retreat back to his junior high's baseball field. He jogged from the Dixie Cream donut shop and made his way to the Woolworth across the street. He discovered a dark corner behind the store near a loading dock, where a pile of cardboard boxes had been discarded. Rusty rummaged through the boxes until he found an empty Maytag box that had been used to hold a washing machine. He crawled inside the large box and tried his best to close the flaps of the box. With his stomach growling, Rusty began shoving the rest of the half-eaten and stale donuts he had saved for later. After having eaten the treats, he cried himself to sleep.

"Told you there was someone in there." Seventeen-year-old Lizzie Johnston whispered to Boo Harper the following morning. They both peered inside the large cardboard box to find a colored boy fast asleep inside.

"Hey, darkie! Get up!" Boo Harper shouted. "You're not allowed back here!"

"Ten more minutes, ma, please?" Rusty replied groggily.

Lizzie gasped as she squinted at his pajamas. "Is that blood?" She asked, covering her mouth with trembling hands. The sudden high-pitch scream of the teenaged girl jolted the boy awake.

"Oh, quit that hollerin'!" Boo demanded, covering his ears.

Startled, Rusty drew further into the box as he stared at Boo and Lizzie in Woolworth uniforms. Any other time, Liz would've asked how his pa, ma, and his schooling were doing. He, in response, would've answered with his usual generic reply. Every time he seen her, he thought about how his ma had told their neighbor that you could always count on Lizzie's ma to bring in the worse meat pie at the annual Toby county fair. Even now, he thought of this.

When Boo had finally gotten Lizzie to quit squawking, she cautiously peered into the opening of the cardboard again and gawked at the colored boy's eyes, which were as deep blue as her own. "It's him! It's him, it's him, it's him!"

Rusty could hear the shrieks of the seventeen-year-old girl as she ran off into the distance. He waited until Boo Harper disappeared from his view, before quickly crawling out the box. He tried sprinting in the opposite direction of the Woolworth but was tackled facedown to the ground by Boo.

"Where do you reckon you're going, spook?" Boo asked, pinning Rusty to the ground. "You're gonna pay for what you've done to the Haynes. Rusty Jr. was one of my best friends." He lied. Boo Harper had always been a bully to Rusty Jr.

"Boo, it's me." Rusty cried out.

Boo narrowed his eyes, then held onto the back of the boy's pajamas as he dragged him to his feet. "What'd you say?"

"I said it's *me*. Rusty."

"How'd you know my name? Were you out here plotting to kill me?!" Boo shouted, looking around the parking lot, suddenly paranoid.

"No!" Rusty assured earnestly. Before he could convince him, Boo kneed him in the stomach. Rusty dropped to his knees as he wrapped his arms around his abdomen. He groaned until his face was met with the sole of Boo's Oxfords.

"Don't cry like a pussy now." Boo snarled, secretly excited to have been the one to capture the Haynes killer.

"Is it him?" Rusty heard the approaching voice of another teenaged boy. He recognized him as the oldest brother of one of his classmates. His name was Charles but everyone in town called him Seven on account of him being born with only seven fingers. He had all five fingers on his right hand, and only his middle and index finger on his left.

"It's the sonofabitch all right." Boo confirmed.

"Sheriff's on his way. Said to be careful. He's considered armed and very dangerous."

"Don't look very dangerous to me." Boo said, as they both looked down at the crying boy.

"We oughta kill this sonofabitch." Seven taunted.

24

Boo chuckled. "Might as well. 'Bout as worthless as tits on a bull, you ask me." He said, before hawking a wad of phlegm at the boy's face.

Seven laughed as Rusty wiped the mucus off of his tear-stained cheeks. Seven, like Boo, couldn't help feeling a rush of excitement at finding the Haynes killer. He knew he'd finally be on the seven o'clock news. He'd always wanted to be on television.

"Can you hold on to 'em while I hit the bushes?" Boo asked. "Been holding it in since I got to work."

Seven nodded, grabbing the boy's arm with his good hand. "Go 'head and drain yer lizard, Boo. I got 'em."

"You sure?" Boo asked tentatively.

"I got it. Go on." Seven reassured.

Boo finally released his grip on Rusty's flannel shirt. Rusty and Seven both watched as he jogged towards some nearby bushes.

"This is all one big mix up. Please let me go." Rusty immediately pleaded.

"Now why would I go and do something like that? The Haynes trailer was right across from ours. Could've been us." Seven replied. "Them pigs are fixin' to skin you alive, darkie, and I'm lookin' forward to watchin'. I think I hear 'em now." He said, looking over his shoulder, towards the direction of the wailing police sirens.

"That sirens I hear?" Boo asked, drawing near.

Without another word, Rusty swiftly clamped down as hard as he could on the teen's forearm.

"Ow!" Seven shouted, rubbing his arm. No sooner had he released his grasp on his pajamas, did Rusty take off running.

"Hey! Come back here!" Seven shouted after him. He and Boo took off running after the boy, but Rusty, running on pure adrenaline, was too quick.

C H A P T E R
S I X

With her thin wrinkled hands trembling, Margaret Browne touched her face. Her eyes were stretched wide in shock as she stared at her mahogany-colored hands, then at her reflection. Her hair was still an awful blue, but it sat on her head in a low tightly coiled afro.

"Lord." Was all she could say, although she kept her mouth open.

She had been standing there inside her bathroom for the past twenty minutes without an inkling of what she should do next. She had no one she could call. Her housekeeper, Charlene, was downstairs tidying up the living room and would be upstairs any minute to make the beds.

Mrs. Browne quickly wet one of the decorative scented Avon soaps she kept near the sink. She lathered up her hands, then scrubbed as if her life depended on it. When she rinsed the suds off and saw that her wrinkly hands were still the color of an acorn, she began whimpering.

"Jesus, Mary, and Joseph. What have I done to deserve this?" She whispered.

There was no way she could let anyone see her this way. She had too much pride to call her family physician or the sheriff's office.

Margaret Browne stared into her eyes, as she finally came to a decision. She could only think of one thing to do.

She walked out of the bathroom and stood at the top of the staircase. Making sure she could not be seen, she shouted for the housekeeper to leave for the day.

"But I haven't even started on the upstairs bedrooms." Charlene protested.

Mrs. Browne quickly assured her that it was okay. "You'll still get paid your ninety-five cents for a full day's of work tomorrow. Just git out."

She waited until she heard the back door open and shut before heading to the attic. She looked around a bit before finally finding what she was looking for.

"Forgive me, Lord." She whispered, heading back to her bedroom.

CHAPTER
SEVEN

His plan was to find the nearest public rotary so he could phone his sister, Julia, in California. Even if he hated the fact that his sister had married a darkie, she was all he had left.

Rusty still remembered it like it was yesterday when she had run off with Seymour Montgomery just two years ago. In fact, it had been him who had found the letter from Julia on the refrigerator one early Friday morning.

"*Ma! Pa!*" He had shouted, running to his parent's room, with the letter still in his hand.

"Would you quit all that hollerin'?" Mr. Haynes bellowed, appearing from the bathroom.

"Where are ya shoes, Russ?" Mrs. Haynes asked, staring at her reflection as she slipped on her dentures. "School bus is fixin' to come any minute now."

"Julia's run away!" Rusty exclaimed, thrusting the letter towards his mother.

"Let me see that." Mr. Haynes said, snatching the letter from his wife's hands. He quickly read the letter. "I'm gonna kill that sonofabitch."

"What? What is it Russell?" Mrs. Haynes asked, slightly panicked. She looked over her husband's shoulder as she attempted to read the letter to the best of her third-grade education. "*California?*" She cried.

Mr. Haynes balled his hands into a fist, crushing the letter. "I'm gonna kill that nigger! Russ, fetch me my rifle!"

Rusty immediately ran out to retrieve his father's Remington.

"Russell, what are ya' fixin to do? We don't know where she is!" Judy cried.

"We don't, but I reckon the Montgomerys must know where their ape son has taken Julia hostage! *Rusty! Hurry up with my gun!*"

Of course, the Montgomerys didn't have a clue as to where Seymour and Julia had run off to. He hadn't even left them a note. The whole thing had been such a big ordeal in Saint Molasses, that the Haynes had convinced the sheriff to arrest Nadine and John Montgomery and their two teenaged boys, in an attempt to get them to confess. The Montgomerys were later released after all of the colored towns people had taken to protesting outside of the sheriff's office a week later for fourteen days straight.

Rusty was brought back to the present at the sight of a public rotary in front of O'Mallard's Laundry Queen. The establishment, usually bustling with whining children, mothers, and housekeepers, was now dark and empty.

Rusty looked over his shoulder and his surroundings, before bolting across the parking lot to the phone booth. He told the operator to connect him to his sister and prayed he had remembered her number correctly.

Someone answered but it wasn't his sister. It was a man with a deep voice.

"Montgomery residence." The man said.

"Is-is this the number to Julia Haynes?" Rusty whispered.

"You've reached the Montgomery residence."

Confused, Rusty repeated, "Is this Julia's number?"

"Yes, yes. This is her husband. Who is this?"

"I need to speak to Julia!" He cried out in hysteria.

"Alright, alright. Hold on." He answered, sensing the caller's urgency.

Rusty Jr. heard him call out to Julia. Then heard Julia ask, "Who is it now?", before grabbing the phone.

"Julia!" Rusty shouted, "It's Rusty!"

"Rusty?" Julia shrieked. "Where are-"

Before Julia could finish, Rusty Haynes Jr, had been knocked out cold. He crumpled to the ground unconscious as the attacker gently placed the phone back on its cradle.

CHAPTER

EIGHT

It started with the blood-curdling screams. Georgia's blood-curdling screams to be exact and it sounded like it was coming from their bathroom.

Jimmy checked the clock on the nightstand. It was barely five in the morning. He willed himself to get up to check on his screaming wife. It wasn't that he didn't care, but he knew how melodramatic Georgia could get. Like a week ago, when Jimmy found her screaming on top of the kitchen table on her hands and knees. When asked what was the matter, she had pointed at the floor blubbering about a trail of red ants.

"Jimmy! Jimmy, help!" He heard her yell.

He flung the sheets off him and shuffled to the adjoining bathroom. He opened the door and nearly jumped out of his skin when he found a tall beautiful mahogany woman, with a large blonde afro in his bathroom. She was also nude.

He stumbled backward. "I'm-I'm sorry. I didn't realize-"

"*It's me.*" The woman said.

Jimmy quickly exited the bathroom and shut the door behind him. Confused, he walked to the living room in search of his wife.

"*Georgiaaa?*" He sang throughout the dining room and kitchen. He wanted to ask why she hadn't warned him about their visitor. "*Where are ya'?*"

"I'm right here, you dingbat!"

"Where?" He asked, following her voice.

The colored woman, still nude, jumped out at him. "Right here!" She cried. *"It's me!"*

She tried to lean her brown body into his, but he held her by the shoulders, away from him. "Don't you think this is inappropriate? What would my wife think? *Georgia!*"

"It's me, Jimmy!" She cried out. "'Look at my eyes!"

For the first time, he studied her eyes. The woman did have blue eyes, just like his wife. "Who are you?" He repeated.

Georgia crumpled to the floor as she wept. "I don't know what's going on. I got up to relieve myself and-and-looked in the mirror. Thought someone else was in the bathroom with me but-but then caught sight of my hands. *Oh gawwd!*" She let out a deafening sob. "I'm a nigger!"

Jimmy cringed, now convinced that the woman was indeed his wife. "How did this happen? What'd you do?"

She leapt to her feet and poked at his chest angrily. "You think I did-" She looked down at her body in disgust. "This? I don't know what happened!" She cried.

This time he took her naked body into his arms. "Think we should call the police?"

She pulled away from him. "The police? I don't want anyone seeing me like *this!*"

He pulled her back onto him. "Calm down, Georgia. We at least need to call Dr. Grier to take a look at you. Suppose this is some type of side effect?"

"Side of effect of *what*?" She asked, pulling away again.

"I don't know. Maybe those Avon cosmetic beauty things you and Eugenia are always wearing or maybe something you ate?"

33

She pushed away in frustration as she shouted, "Something I ate?!" She walked over to the full-length mirror behind the door and stared at herself as she cried.

He sighed. "Honey, I don't know! All's I'm saying is we need to have this checked out. There may have been other reports of the same symptom. We don't know."

"You think I'm dying?!"

"Did you hear me say you were dying, woman!" He shouted back.

She tugged at the loose coils on her head. "Just look at my hair!"

Jimmy studied his wife. He thought his wife still looked beautiful, exotic almost, even as a colored woman.

Don't ever forget. He could hear the boy's voice in his head.

Jimmy stared at her for a few seconds longer, tempted to reveal his long-held secret. "Get dressed. I'm gonna phone Dr. Grier."

"No!" She exclaimed. "Get the colored doctor. Montgomery."

Jimmy raised a brow. "Montgomery?"

"I can't let anyone see me like this!" She barked.

"So, you *don't* want me to phone Dr. Montgomery?" He asked, confused.

"Mr. Montgomery is colored. That's different."

"Alright, I'll get the phone book."

" Oh no. *No, no, no, no!*" She wailed.

"What? What is it?"

"Eugenia is fixin to pick me up in a couple of hours in her brand-new Cadillac."

"Just call her up and tell 'er you can't make it. You don't have to tell 'er what's goin' on."

Georgia wept as she explained. "But the grand opening of the new Belk in Marmalade is this morning! Now what am I gonna do?"

Jimmy gathered his sobbing wife into his arms. "Calm down, Georgia. I'll call Dr. Montgomery right away. I'm sure he'll be able to tell us what's going on and fix this."

"You think he'll be able to heal me before 9?" Georgia sniffled.

"I'll call him right now and ask."

She looked up at him with wet eyes. "And if he can't make it on account of other appointments, just offer to pay him a day's wages in cash." She urged.

"I'll do everything I can, Georgia. Don't worry." Jimmy assured.

CHAPTER
NINE

"*I know he's still alive. I heard his voice with my own ears and so did my husband. Please, I'm begging, if anyone has any information, please contact the authorities. Other than my husband, Seymour, and our daughter, Rusty's the only family I've got left. I love you, Rusty. I'm gonna do everything I can to find you.*"

"Bet it was someone kin to Seymour who done it." Earline Thompson predicted, clicking off the tabletop television on top of the kitchen counter.

She placed a bowl of steaming oatmeal on the table. "Be careful out there," Earline advised, "That murderer is still out there somewhere."

"Don't worry, we'll catch him." Detective Dylan Ford assured his long-time girlfriend. "We'll turn every one of those coloreds' houses upside-down if we need to. He's gotta be still in town hiding out somewhere. There's only one way in and out of Molasses and Sheriff Woods' already set up a police checkpoint on highway 11."

Truthfully, this double homicide and missing person's case had been the most excitement Toby county had had in over a decade. There hadn't been a serious crime committed since the mid-fifties and that had involved the death of Margaret Browne's French poodle, Bambi.

Earline stood behind the detective and began massaging his shoulders. "Have you told her yet?'

"Told what to who?' He asked gruffly. He knew exactly who she was talking about, but he wasn't in the mood to argue. Especially not this morning.

"Moriah. Have you told 'er?"

"I'm getting to it, Earline. Just hold ya' britches, will ya?"

Earline removed her hands from the detective's shoulder. Well if you won't' tell her, I will."

Dylan looked over his shoulder at her. "You let me handle it, alright?"

"I've been waiting on you to handle it for the past six years, Dylan. Now this baby is fixin' to come out in another six months whether you like it or not. If I don't see any divorce papers by the end of this month, all hell is fixin' to break loose. Ya' hear me?"

Ignoring her threats, he asked, "Where's my coffee?" He knew as long as he continued paying her rent and her bills, she wasn't going anywhere. Besides, he couldn't just leave his wife and their three children.

She walked over to the coffee maker, poured him out a cup of coffee, and slammed it on the table in front of him, spilling some on the table. He shook his head as he watched Earline storm out of the kitchen before he could thank her for breakfast. A few seconds later, he cringed when he heard her bedroom door slam shut.

∗∗∗

"Rough morning?" Detective Edward Bailey asked his partner half an hour later, lowering the volume of the radio inside the blue unmarked Dodge Monaco.

Detective Ford took in a deep breath from the passenger seat. "Just Earline bitchin' again."

As usual, Bailey decided not to speak on his partner's marital affairs. It was something he couldn't fathom doing to his own wife, Shelby.

"Any new leads?' Ford asked.

"Margaret Browne was just reported missing 'bout half an hour ago."

"Missing?" Detective Ford repeated. "Who reported it?" He asked, knowing the old woman lived alone and had no children.

"The maid." Bailey answered. "And that's not even the strangest part."

Detective Ford looked over at his partner. "There's more?"

"An unidentified colored woman was found hanging from the ceiling fan in Mrs. Browne's bedroom."

"Think it might be connected to the Haynes' case?"

"Might be. Seems like that's the killer's M.O. He kills and kidnaps."

"Downright strange. If it is the same killer, why would he kill a white couple the first time and a nigger the second time? Housekeeper see anything?"

"Don't know yet." Bailey answered.

"Gotta be the same killer as the Haynes. Never been so many heinous crimes committed in a single week."

"That's why we need to speak to the maid." Bailey pointed out.

"Who's the maid?"

"Charlene McGwire."

"Oh great. The McGwires." Ford rolled his eyes, then continued, "Guess that mean we gotta drive to the fuckin' south side."

"I ain't too happy about driving to the ghetto either, but somebody's gotta do it." Baily said.

The two men were interrupted by their police radio. Another kidnapping had taken place at Meadowbrook Square, the trailer park community.

Bailey swiftly made a U-turn, heading back in the direction he had just picked up Ford. "Looks like we're headed back to your neck of the woods."

"Not in the least." Ford disagreed. "My neck of the woods is over on the north side where Moriah and the kids are. Livin' situation is just temporary."

Bailey chuckled, not bothering to tell Ford that he already knew the truth. Word had spread like wildfire a couple of months back, that Moriah Ford had kicked her husband out of their plush two-story home after learning of his affair with Earline Thompson.

They pulled up to the trailer to find uniformed officers and an ambulance in front of the trailer. They also found Lizzie Johnston in her Woolworth uniform standing outside, trying her best to console her six-year-old sister, Charlotte Johnston.

"You gals alright?" Detective Bailey asked, as Detective Ford walked past to check out the crime scene.

"She shot daddy!" Charlotte cried, pointing up at her older sister.

"How many times do I gotta tell ya, Charlotte? I didn't shoot daddy!"

"Is he missing?" Bailey asked, retrieving his notepad.

Lizzie nodded. "I was getting ready for work and-" Her voice trailed off as she began crying.

"He's not missing." Charlotte interjected. "He just looks different."

"Different? Bailey repeated.

Before she could answer, Detective Ford returned. "Suspect's still alive." He revealed to Bailey. "Apparently, Lizzie here saved the family by shooting the bastard right in the gut. 'Atta girl."

"My daddy's not a bastard!" Charlotte shouted angrily.

Ford knelt down in front of the six-year-old. "I wasn't talkin' 'bout yer pops, Buttercup. I was talkin' 'bout the colored man inside."

"That's my daddy!" Charlotte hollered.

"I'm sorry, detectives." Lizzie apologized. "I reckon she's still a bit traumatized."

"'Can you tell us exactly what happened?" Bailey asked.

Lizzie nodded. "I woke up this morning, took a shower and brushed my teeth, and got dressed for work like I do every mornin'. While I was fixin' my hair, I heard Charlotte, here, laughin' in my pa's room. I really didn't think nothin' of it. My pa usually drives me to work every morning. So I go in his room to tell 'em that I'm ready to go and some strange nigger is rubbing on my sister."

"He weren't rubbing on me! He was tickling me." Charlotte corrected.

"Doesn't matter none." Lizzie snapped at Charlotte. "He's a stranger and a colored one at that!"

"But he isn't a stranger." Charlotte protested.

"Charlotte, hush! I don't wanna hear another word." Lizzie instructed. She returned her attention back to the detectives. "Anyway, soon as the nigger sees me, he calls out my name."

"He said your name?" Ford inquired.

She nodded. "And he was wearing my pa's pajamas. I 'mmediately grabbed Charlotte and told her to run next door to Renee's trailer. I didn't wanna leave daddy in there with the nigger, so I grabbed daddy's huntin' rifle from the cupboards and-" The teen broke into tears as she tried to continue.

40

"Take 'yer time." Bailey consoled.

"I heard daddy in the room yelling frantically. So I rushed in there with the rifle but didn't see him. All's I seen was the nigger in front of the dresser mirror shouting and touching his hair. So I did what I felt I had to do at that moment. I shot 'em."

"Do you have any idea how he might've gotten in?" Ford asked. "They aren't finding any signs of forced entry."

Lizzie shook her head.

"And you said he knew your name?" Bailey asked.

"Yes, he said my name. I'm sure of it."

"Did his face look familiar at all? Like you might've seen him at work or somethin'?" Bailey asked.

"I don't know. I don't think so." She replied. Then her eyes lit up. "Yesterday behind the Woolworth, Boo and I seen another strange nigger sleeping in a box. He had blue eyes like the Haynes' murderer. Maybe he sent one of his killer buddies to find me for blabbing to the law?"

"The Haynes murderer?" Bailey asked, glancing at Ford.

She nodded. "We called the sheriff's office, but he ran off before the police arrived."

"And you're saying you suspect the nigger who broke in your trailer this morning is in cahoots with the Haynes killer?" Ford asked.

"I think so. I think they might've kidnapped daddy for revenge!"

"No!" Charlotte suddenly cried out in frustration. "*That's daddy! You shot daddy!*" The six-year-old repeated.

CHAPTER

T EN

"This fool's knocked out cold." Fifteen-year-old Malcolm McGwire whispered.

Noah McGwire, his older brother by two years, shrugged. "He'll be alright." He said nonchalantly.

"He looks dead." Marley said, thumb in mouth. At just seven-years-old, he was the youngest of the McGwire boys.

"Say, big brother, what'd you hit 'em with? A bat?" Ida McGwire inquired. From a distance, most people couldn't tell that the chubby fourteen-year-old was a girl. The youngest daughter of Frank and Yvette McGwire's six children, she had ditched dresses and skirts in the second grade. To her mother's disdain, Ida played just as rough and got just as dirty as her three brothers.

"I clocked him with my sock of rocks." Noah informed. "The sucka ain't dead."

The four McGwire children stood inside their parents' shed, surrounding the unconscious body soiled with blood.

With his thumb still in his mouth, Marley inspecting the boy's afro. "I've never seen a negro with red hair before."

"You think it's him?" Ida asked her older brothers.

"We won't know til he comes to." Noah answered.

"It's gotta be the killer. Look at his threads." Ida said, eyeing his soiled pajamas.

42

Malcolm looked at Noah, "What's the point in finding out when he wakes up? All we gotta do is check his eyes."

Ida nodded. "That's right. They said the killer had blue eyes." She nudged her youngest brother. "Check his eyes, Marley."

Marley took a few steps back. He gave his thumb a break as he whimpered, "I don't wanna touch a dead body."

"He's not dead." Noah repeated. He looked at Malcolm. "It was your idea. You check."

"You found 'em." Malcolm shot back.

"You boys are a bunch of pussies. I'll do it." Ida offered. "But first, I need you boys to tie him up."

Noah nodded and immediately instructed his two younger brothers to find some rope.

Part of the reason Noah had knocked out the boy at the payphone was the reward money. He and his two older sisters were forced to drop out of school after their father's mishap with a forklift at work. The accident had left their father, who had never missed a day of work, a paraplegic. Without his income as a warehouse worker, their mother had gone back to work as a nanny for the middle-class white folks over on the north side of Molasses.

The sight of a crying Julia Haynes-Montgomery being comforted by her colored husband on television, was all the residents of Saint Molasses and nearby cities could talk about. The majority, including the coloreds, were so disgusted by the outright public display of affection, they had barely heard a word she'd said about the thousand-dollar reward for any information leading to the discovery of her brother, Rusty Jr. Noah had recognized the thin colored man seated with Julia on his television screen. Seymour Montgomery had once dated his eldest sister, Savannah, back in junior high. Seymour's pa, Dr. Montgomery, was also the McGwire's family physician.

"We found something better than rope." Malcolm said, entering the shed. He held out a long heavy chain with a lock attached. It was the same thick chain that Noah had used to secure his bike to the Magnolia tree out front, that is, until his bike was stolen a few weeks ago.

"Sweet!" Noah exclaimed. He chained Rusty's hands and legs just as Rusty began to stir.

The McGwire children watched as the boy groaned in pain. Their mouths parted open as he groaned, slowly opening his eyelids.

"*Heeeelp!*" Rusty hollered.

"Say, hand me the duct tape, baby brother." Ida instructed Marley. She looked over at Rusty, who was still hollering for help. "You must be all kinds of stupid yellin' and carryin' on like this." Ida knelt down and stretched out a line of duct tape in front of the boy's face. "Now, are you ready to cooperate or will I need to shut that big mouth of yours?"

"Let me go!" Rusty ordered. "Or I'll call the sheriff on you apes!"

Malcolm and Noah erupted in laughter.

"Go right ahead. Call 'em." Noah said. "Those honkies will fry you faster than a bucket of chicken."

"This clown must have mush for brains." Malcolm half-joked. "Either that or Mr. Haynes beat 'em so bad, he gave 'em amnesia."

With his nostrils flaring, Rusty could barely contain his rage. He was outraged at the way he was being treated, as if *he* were one of *them*, as if they didn't know their place.

"Don't you think we should call the sheriff?" Marley asked, thumb in mouth.

Noah rubbed his hands together as he thought about the reward money. "Soon." He answered.

"Shouldn't we find out why he killed them first?" Malcolm asked.

Ida glared at Malcolm. "Does it matter?"

"Matters to me." Malcolm answered, remembering the time Mr. Haynes had threatened to shoot their father a few years back for taking the last *good* Christmas tree at the tree farm.

"It's not like this fool's gonna tell us the truth no how." Ida pointed out.

"What's your name?" Marley asked innocently, taking a closer look at the fugitive.

"Get away from 'em, Marl." Ida warned, pulling him away.

Frustrated, Rusty scowled. "My ma and pappy is Russell and Judith Haynes. I'd be afraid to keep the son of a high-rankin' klans member hostage, if I were you." The children erupted in laughter.

Malcolm spoke up first. "Say, that Mr. Haynes must've really did a number on you right before you killed 'em."

"Yeah," Ida chuckled, "Everyone knows he beat his wife. Did he bust you upside ya' nappy head, too?"

"That's a lie!" Rusty shouted. "My pappy never laid a hand on my ma." He lied. He wasn't about to air out his family's dirty laundry to a bunch of spooks.

"Never met a nigga who talk just like those hillbillies over at Meadowbrook." Ida laughed. "This clown is definitely shuckin' and jivin' right now. Trying to make a fool of us."

"This fool really think he kin to white folks." Noah said, chuckling. "I think I must've hit 'em harder than I thought."

Marley took a step closer to the fugitive-turned-hostage. "What's your name?"

"Rusty." He answered sourly.

Noah, Malcolm, and Ida all held up their hands in the air as they guffawed.

"*I am Rusty!*" He cried out.

"And I'm Paul Newman." Noah teased, causing the siblings to hoot in laughter.

"I'm Julie Andrews." Ida chimed. "Better yet, call me Marilyn Monroe." Ida said seductively.

"Well just call me John Wayne." Malcolm said.

"I am Rusty! Let me loose! Let me outta here!"

"Well, I warned you 'bout all that hollerin'." Ida said. She stretched out a long strip of tape and covered his mouth, as her brothers continued to laugh at the boy's delirium.

CHAPTER

ELEVEN

D r. John Montgomery was trying to decide if it were possible to transport both Jimmy Daniels and his negro *mistress* to an asylum. He wondered where Mrs. Daniels was this early in the morning. Everyone knew that the white women on the north side of town were housewives. He suddenly felt uncomfortable. He didn't want to have anything to do with Mr. Daniel's apparent infidelity.

"With all due respect, sir," The doctor said to Jimmy, who seemed like the least crazy of the two. "I can't help you. I'm sorry."

Dr. Montgomery stood to his feet just as the negro woman fell to her knees. "Please, Mr. Montgomery!" She pleaded.

"That's *Dr.* Montgomery." He corrected.

"Please, you can't leave me like this!"

He shook his head in pity at the woman. This was the reason why he was so against interracial relations. Eventually, these self-hating colored men and women swore they were white folks trapped in negro bodies. "Listen, sista, I can't help you!" He snapped.

"Now wait just a doggone minute." Jimmy glared at the physician. "Who do you think you are speakin' to her that way?"

Dr. Montgomery grabbed his medicine bag and stood in front of Jimmy. "With all due respect, Mr. Daniels, maybe it

47

would help if she went back *to her own kind.*" He suggested, thinking of his eldest son, Seymour, who had run off to San Francisco with a white girl two years ago.

"What in the hell is that supposed to mean? Her own kind?" Jimmy spat.

Dr. Montgomery's jaws clenched. "You know," He said boldly, "A *negro.*"

Glowering, Jimmy took a step towards the angry old man. "I *am* a *negro!* My mother's colored!"

"Your mother's a nigger?" asked Georgia.

The doctor, fed up with the couple's delusion, stormed out of the two-story home.

Georgia stood to her feet. "I'm married to a nig-?" Before Georgia could finish, Jimmy slapped her.

"Do *not* call me a nigger."

Her cheek felt as if it were on fire. She put her hand up to her face. "You hit me." She stated, dazed.

"I'm-I'm sorry." For a moment Jimmy's heart pounded at the realization at what he'd just done. Not only had he just struck a woman, something he was taught to never do, but a *white* woman at that. All Georgia had to do was call the law and tell 'em that he was a colored, and his ass would be grass.

"I'm so sorry." He repeated.

Georgia took a step towards him and landed a powerful slap onto his face in return. "I'm calling the police!"

"Have you looked at yourself lately?" He asked her, remembering himself that she couldn't go to the law. They would immediately have her committed.

"I can't believe you've lied to me all these years!" She shouted. "Is this why I've never met your family? Why we've never gone to Dayton?"

Don't you ever forget where you came from, Jimmy. There was that voice in his head again.

"Yes." Jimmy admitted.

Georgia's blue eyes filled with tears. She pointed a finger in his face. "I want a divorce." She said calmly.

He felt as if he'd just been stabbed in the chest. "You really want a divorce?"

Ignoring her husband, Georgia marched towards their bedroom in tears. He could hear her throwing god-knows-what against the wall in a rage.

Jimmy placed both his hands on his head, as he tried to calm himself. *This is crazy.* He thought. That whole week, starting from when he'd met that peculiar fella, had felt surreal. His thoughts were suddenly interrupted by a series of knocks on his front door. He looked out the peep hole and nearly soiled himself when he seen Dylan Ford and Edward Bailey standing outside his door.

Jimmy hurriedly shot up the stairs to their bedroom, where he found Georgia flinging articles of clothing in a brown bulky suitcase in a haste. "Georgia-"

"Don't you dare speak my name! I don't know who you are." She scowled.

"Look Georgia, I need you to stay upstairs."

"I am *leaving*, Jimmy, and don't you dare try to stop me!"

He walked over to where she stood and grabbed her by the shoulders. "Listen to me-"

"Get your paws off me."

He quickly released her shoulders. "The cops are downstairs-"

"*Good!*" She spat, returning her attention to her luggage.

49

"Just stay upstairs, Georgia!" He instructed sternly before making his way out the bedroom. Half-way down the stair-case, Jimmy ran back up the stairs and grabbed the wooden chair from out the guest bedroom. He could still hear the faint sounds of pounding downstairs, as he propped the chair underneath the knob of the bedroom door, so that the door would not open.

Jimmy fled down the stairs two steps at a time. Out of breath, he flung the door open and smiled at the detectives.

Detective Bailey smiled. "We were just about to call in a search party."

Detective Ford glanced at his partner, then at Jimmy. "Are you alright? Sweatin' like a hog there, Jimbo."

"Just outta shape. Can't run down the stairs as easily as I used to." Jimmy smiled awkwardly. "Is there something I can help you fellas with?"

"We need to ask you some questions. Don't worry, yer not in any trouble or anything." Detective Ford said. "Mind if we come in?"

Jimmy glanced up the stairs then back at the officers. "I'm..uh... not feeling too well."

"We'll make this quick." Detective Bailey reassured.

With a sigh of defeat, Jimmy stepped aside to allow the detectives in. They both sat down on the floral-print sofa while Jimmy remained standing.

"Is the missus in?" Ford inquired nonchalantly. He had always thought of Georgia Daniels as the sexiest piece of tail in Saint Molasses. Just the thought of her long legs, deep blue eyes, and curly blonde hair was enough to arouse him.

"Yeah, sh-she's upstairs." He stammered. "How can I help you fellas?"

"Not sure if you've heard," Bailey began, "Margaret Browne is missing."

Jimmy took a seat on the armchair across from the officers, as the detectives explained how Mrs. Browne had suggested they speak to Jimmy about the peculiar stranger she'd seen in front of Brook's Pharmacy before she went missing.

Bailey retrieved his pen and notepad from inside his suit jacket. "Do you remember the conversation you had with the boy?"

The sound of clunking and thumping from upstairs startled both Jimmy and the detectives. Jimmy knew then that Georgia was attempting to open the bedroom door.

"Jimmy! You sonofabitch!" They heard Georgia holler.

Both of Detective Ford's brows rose.

"We were kinda in the middle of somethin'." Jimmy explained.

"Ahh." Ford smiled, assuming he was speaking of *adult* relations.

Jimmy continued, "As far as the colored fella at Brook's Pharmacy, he didn't say much. Just wanted directions to the nearest motel."

"What'd you tell 'em?" Bailey questioned, scribbling on his pad.

Jimmy furrowed his brow. "Can't remember. Think I might've suggested he go on to Marmalade."

"Can you describe what he had on?" Ford asked.

"Jimmy! Let me out!" Georgia hollered.

"Uh- just a minute, honey! I'll be right up!" Jimmy shouted. He gave the detectives an apologetic smile. "What were you saying?"

"His clothes." Bailey repeated.

He shook his head. "I don't recall."

51

"Mrs. Browne said he was driving an automobile. Do you remember seeing him in one?" Ford questioned.

"Jimmy! You sonofabitch! Are you there?!" Georgia shouted, followed by a loud thump, then a crash.

Jimmy's cheeks turned a deep crimson. "I'm sorry detectives, now's not a good time. Maybe we can do this another time?" He asked nervously, standing to his feet.

The detectives also stood. Bailey extended a card to Jimmy. "How about we stop by again tomorrow? In the meantime, give us a call if you remember anything."

"That sounds fine. I'll do that." Jimmy nodded before leading the men to the door.

"One more thing," Ford said, once they were all standing outside. "Don't open the door for any niggers even if you recognize 'em. We're not sure if Mrs. Browne's disappearance had anything to do with her speaking to us."

Jimmy rose a brow. "Is me and my wife in danger?"

"We haven't got all the facts yet." Bailey explained. "We don't know if the Hayne's killer is also the kidnapper or if there's some type of operation goin' on. Like we said, we're advising you and your wife to use precaution."

Jimmy nodded.

"Be safe." Ford said before him and his partner headed back to the blue Monaco.

Jimmy took in a deep breath and returned to his two-story home just as Georgia was stomping down the stairs with a brown leather suitcase. She wore a yellow long-sleeved dress that fell to her ankles and her hair was wrapped in a black scarf.

"Georgia-" Jimmy called out.

"How dare you try to keep me hostage. I'm leaving. I can't bear to stay another minute in this house. Hell, I can't stay another minute in this god forsaken town!"

Jimmy stepped in front of her, blocking her path to the door. "Georgia. We can leave together. Just give me enough time for me to save some money and sell the house." He pleaded.

She stomped her feet and glowered at him. "I'm not staying anywhere with *you*!"

"Georgia." He whispered.

"Get out my way." She barked, shoving him aside.

CHAPTER

TWELVE

"As Mayor of Saint Molasses, I assure you I will get to the bottom of this. We are searching high and low for all of your missing loved ones. As of today, we have jailed approximately seven intruders, all nonresidents of this town. As a precaution, we have set a mandatory curfew for all negroes. Effective immediately, all negroes caught outside after 6 p.m. will be jailed. All negroes coming to and from work, must provide a signed note from their employer. We are asking all residents of Saint Molasses to keep all windows shut and doors locked. We are also asking all residents to stay indoor in groups if possible. Again, we do not recommend that anyone stay indoors alone."

"Just a shame, isn't it?" Shirley Dalton asked her two younger neighbors, as they all stared at the black-and-white tabletop television sitting on her neighbor's kitchen counter.

"Heard Julia Hayne's 'posed to be coming all the way from California to help look for her brother." Earline informed.

Shirley nodded. "Heard the same thing. She'd better be careful if she does. Who's to say the killer won't go huntin' her down next once she's here?"

Penny Thorton shook her long mousy hair at the television screen as she sipped from a frosted beer mug. "Raymond and I are fixin' to get us a big ol' watchdog."

"What's a watchdog gonna do if those sonofabitches have guns?" Shirley asked.

"I dare one of them niggers to break in my trailer." Earline snarled. "Gotta shot gun right underneath my bed and a pistol under my pillow."

"Not to mention, a cute detective you're sleepin' with." Penny giggled. "Almost as handsome as that Robert Redford."

Earline smiled. "Dylan's alright, I guess."

"Well, it's bad enough my nephew, Boo, is being drafted." Shirley Dalton vented, wishing she hadn't forgotten to bring her pack of Virginia Slims. "Now we gotta deal with these niggers. How 'bout Nixon pack 'em all up and ship 'em over to 'Nam to die in the fuckin' war?"

"Yer sure you don't want a drink?" Penny asked Earline.

Earline waved a hand dismissively in the air. "Nah, trying to cut back." She lied. She wasn't ready to tell her neighbors that she was pregnant by the married detective. It was bad enough that word had gotten to Moriah Ford about the affair a few months ago after another neighbor, Renee Thatcher, had caught Dylan sneaking out of Earline's trailer one early morning.

"Wanna know who I think is ta' blame for all of this mess?" Shirley asked before taking a swig from her bottle of Busch.

"Who?" Earline asked, interest piqued.

"That damn Black Panther gang what's got them niggers so bold. Think they can just come 'ere and terrorize our town."

"Funny you should say that," Earline began. "I was telling Dylan just yesterday that I wouldn't be surprised if those Black Panthers was behind all this."

"The Black Panther Party?" Penny asked. "I don't see why'd they come to a little ol' town like Molasses. Most people don't even know this town exist."

Shirley scowled at Penny. "Use your brain, Penny. That's what they want you to think. That's how they operate."

Earline nodded in agreement. "Wanna know who else I think is to blame?" She asked.

"Kennedy." Shirley replied matter-of-factly.

"Good one." Earline responded. "Him too, but I was talkin' about that reporter from Texas. I forget his name. Y'all remember him?"

Penny furrowed her brows in confusion.

Earline stared at Penny. "You know, the white newspaper writer who made national headlines couple years ago?"

Shirley lifted both hands in the air as she huffed, "Newspaper writer?" They both knew Shirley could barely read a recipe, let alone the paper.

Penny's eyes lit up. "'Are you talkin' about John Griffith? Or was it Griffin?"

Earline immediately snapped her fingers. "That's it! John Howard Griffin. The nigger-lover. Went undercover as a nigger and wrote about it. Did a bunch of horse shit interviews about how he thought they should be treated different."

"Well I don't think they're all that bad. Not all of 'em." Penny confessed.

Earline scoffed. "Oh, *puh-leeze!*"

"What about Dorothy Dandridge and Ray Charles?" Penny asked. She was also tempted to point out the time they had all guffawed non-stop during Richard Pryor's stand-up routine on the Ed Sullivan Show a couple of weeks back.

Earline rolled her eyes.

"And that other one," Penny continued, "Billie Holiday? Are they all bad?"

"That's different." Earline said defensively. "Just because I like those people's music or movies, don't mean I like 'em. Besides, them's are rich coloreds."

Shirley nodded. "Them rich ones got some good sense."

Feeling her anxiety rising, Penny opted to drop the issue. Before moving to Meadowbrook Square, she had grown up with negroes. She still remembered her childhood friend, Tosha Larkins, whom she had always thought was beautiful. She would never admit it to the other ladies, but she had even gotten knocked up once by a colored boy from the south side. It had taken Penny two whole weeks to find an underground abortionist, and another two weeks to scrounge up the fifty-dollars to have the illegal abortion performed on top of a wobbly dining room table.

"You better never let Ray hear you talk like that." Shirley advised Penny.

Earline nodded. "Better never let *me* hear you talk like that again neither." She threatened.

"Good lord," Shirley said, scowling at the image of Julia and Seymour Montgomery on the television screen. "I am just so sick and tired of seeing their long faces every time I turn on the gotdamn T.V."

Earline nodded. "She knows it's all her fault this whole mess done happened. That's why she can't stop crying."

"How so?" Penny asked.

"If she would've never left and run off with that nigger, none of this would've never happened. It was someone kin to that husband of hers who did it. I guarantee it."

"I like her." Penny admitted. "She was always nice to me."

57

"Who cares?" Shirley grumbled. "I swear, sometimes you two 'mind me of Tweedle Dee and Tweedle Dum."

"Mind yer manners, Shirley." Earline warned. "I ain't nobody's Tweedle Dum or Tweedle Dee."

"Ya know what we should do?" Shirley asked, ignoring Earline.

"What's that?" Penny answered.

"We should organize a neighborhood watch."

"That's a great idea, Shirley."

"That does sound like a good idea." Earline admitted. Ever since she'd quit her job as a cashier at the Piggly Wiggly's, she found herself at home alone often and could use the extra eyes on her trailer. As of late, she didn't get to see Dylan until the wee hours of the morning on account of the Haynes murder/kidnapping case.

"How about we hold a meeting tomorrow night?" Shirley asked. "Penny, I need you to make flyers and pass 'em out door to door."

"Flyers? I don't have enough paper 'round here to make flyers." She protested.

"Well then, knock on everybody's door between today and tomorrow and let em know to meet outside your trailer at seven p.m. sharp if they're interested. Think you can handle that?"

CHAPTER

THIRTEEN

"Say, which one of you called The Man?" Noah shouted to his younger siblings the following evening. He had just emptied a metal bucket they had given Rusty to relieve himself in.

Rusty's blue eyes lit up. "The cops are here?" He asked, straightening his shoulders.

"I didn't call 'em." Ida said, looking through a peephole towards the front of the shed. She saw two plain-clothed officers standing at their front door. "I'll go see what they want." She offered.

Malcolm placed a hand on his younger sister's shoulder. "I'll go. You stay here."

Rusty waited for Malcolm to open the door to the shed, then shouted, *"HELP! HEEEELP!"*

Alarmed, Malcolm immediately shut the door. He made a beeline to their hostage as Rusty continued shouting. Noah gave the boy a kick to the rib, immediately silencing his calls for help as he groaned in agony.

"Hush up, nigga!" Malcolm growled.

Seeing the rage in his brother's eyes, Noah quickly held Malcolm back. "Malcolm, calm down, little brother."

"They're talking to Charlene and Mama." Ida informed, staring out the peephole.

Noah released an air of relief. "Must be 'bout that missin' white woman Charlene worked for."

"Ms. Margaret?" Marley asked, remembering how much his eldest sister always complained about working for the old woman.

"Mrs. Margaret?" Rusty repeated. "She's missing?"

Malcolm frowned at Rusty. "What's it to ya'?"

"She was a good friend of my ma's and pappy." He answered.

Ida walked back over to them. "I heard they found an old colored woman hangin' from her bedroom."

Spooked, Marley held on to his sister's leg.

"Bet they're gonna blame that one on me too." Rusty predicted.

Malcolm stared at Rusty. "Why'd you kill the Haynes?"

"I didn't want to. I had to. It was self-defense. They were gonna kill me!" He admitted, tearfully.

"What'd you do with the Haynes' son?" Noah asked.

Rusty sobbed.

"Did you kill 'em?" Asked Ida.

Marley pulled his thumb out of his mouth. "He *is* Rusty."

Rusty's heart leapt as he stared at Marley. "That's right, Marley."

"Hush, Marl." Ida chastised. "Don't you see grown folks talkin'?"

"He's right." Rusty said. "I *am* Rusty."

Noah huffed in aggravation. "Look, brother, you don't have to tell us anything. I don't care. All I care about is the reward money."

"Can't I have something to eat?" Rusty asked. "I haven't eaten supper in two days."

60

Marley stuffed his hand inside the pocket of his overalls. He pulled out a pack of gummy worms and handed it to the boy.

"You didn't have to give it to him, Marl." Said Ida.

Rusty nodded gratefully at the seven-year-old. "Thank you, Marley."

"Oh my God!" Ida exclaimed. "His pinky! Look at his pinky!"

Malcolm and Noah's mouth fell open as they witnessed both of Rusty's pinky turn to its former pale hue.

"Well, I'll be damned." Malcolm whispered, taking a few steps back.

Rusty's eyes widened with glee. "I told you! I told you!"

Ida and Noah glanced at one another.

"How'd you do that?" Ida queried.

"I dunno. That's what I've been tryin' to explain."

"Can you tell us again, 'bout what happened that morning?" Noah asked, taking a seat on a nearby crate.

An hour came and went as Rusty Jr explained in great detail everything that had led to the deaths of his parent. He answered every question the children asked to best of his knowledge.

"And you say you don't know how this happened?" Noah asked again.

Rusty shook his head as he shrugged his shoulder. "I don't know. It could've happened to just about anybody. It could've happened to either one of ya."

Frightened, Marley held on to his sister.

"I don't know how or why this happened." Rusty continued.

"Maybe somebody put out a hex on you." Malcolm teased, still unconvinced that the boy was who he claimed to be.

"Laugh all ya want, but how else would you explain my finger changin' color?" Rusty pointed out.

"I believe 'em." Ida said.

"So do I." Noah admitted.

Malcolm slapped his knees as he laughed at them. "You fools will believe anything. Well let's just say this clown's telling the truth, how do you know that whatever he's got ain't contagious?"

Noah, Marley, and Ida looked at one another, then quickly moved a couple of feet away from Rusty as Malcolm hooted with laughter.

"Good point." Noah commented.

"This fool is just jivin', ya dig. He'd say anything for us to let 'em free." Malcolm assured.

"I'm tellin' the truth!" Rusty said adamantly.

"Well I believe him." Ida repeated. "You still can't explain his skin changing' color right 'fore our very eyes."

Noah nodded in agreement.

Ida looked at Noah. "Should we let 'em go?"

Malcolm's eyes widened. "Let 'em go? Would you be sayin' the same if you were convinced that he were really a negro? I say we call the law 'fore he restores the rest of his color. It'd look real bad for us to have a cracker chained up. It'd look real bad."

"But he's just a kid." Ida protested. "And he's innocent."

"So was Emmett Till." Malcolm pointed out, scowling. "Those honkies lynched him right here in Mississippi and he was all but fourteen."

Rusty finally spoke up. "That had nothin' to do with me. I wasn't kin to any of those white folks who done it."

"Don't matter." Malcolm replied, crouching to his feet. "Your ma and pops are one of the most racist white folks in all of Toby county. Did you know yer pa once had his neighbor sic his Great Dane on me on account of me walking through the trailer park?"

"Well what'd you expect? Everyone knows coloreds aren't welcomed at Meadowbrook." Rusty said, not understanding what the issue was. If the coloreds did what they ought to do and not do what they ought not to do, there wouldn't be any issues.

Malcolm stared at the ground as he shook his head. He stood up as he explained to Rusty, "See that's the problem right there. You white folks think yer all high and mighty. We all oughta have the same rights. Instead, they print lies about us in the paper and make us out to be savages on the news."

Ida took a step forward. "Malcolm, I agree with everything you just said, but how is turning him in gonna change things?"

"What about the reward money?" Noah asked.

She turned to Noah. "It's just not right and you two know it."

Noah sighed. "We really could use the money. *A whole grand.* You know what we can do with that type of money?"

"We could buy a family car." Malcolm pointed out. "Mama and pops ain't never owned no car."

Noah nodded in agreement. "And I could finally buy me a new pair of shoes. I'm tired of wearing pops hand-me downs."

"I want a Rock 'Em Sock 'Em Robot!" Marley added excitedly.

Malcolm looked at Ida. "You could finally get that big ol' color T.V. you've been gripin' to mama and pops about."

Ida smiled. "I was thinkin' about maybe addin' new baseball cards to my collection."

"You're turning me in?" Rusty asked.

"Looks like it, brutha." Malcolm answered.

"Wait," Ida said. "Can we all agree not to call the law until we sleep on it first?"

Noah nodded. "Fine with me."

Malcolm sighed. "Alright. Fine, but tomorrow we'll take a vote on it." He said, already confident he'd have his way.

CHAPTER
FOURTEEN

"Whatcha' think?" Detective Ford asked, backing the blue Dodge Monaco out of the McGwire's front yard.

"Sounds identical to the Dalton case." Bailey replied, referring to the colored woman who had been found hanging inside the bedroom closet in Shirley Dalton's trailer. Like the other cases, Shirley had also been reported missing by her adult son, Scooter Dalton.

"We need to hurry up and make an arrest. The FBI is threatening to step in if we don't close this case soon." Ford informed.

Bailey stared out of the window pensively.

"What's on your mind?" Ford queried, glancing at his partner.

"Nothing really." Bailey replied, looking straight ahead. "I mean...isn't it a bit odd that all of the colored intruders we've caught alive inside the homes insisted that they were...." Bailey allowed his voice to trail off before he could finish, realizing how insane his thoughts would sound.

"What? What is it?" Ford pressed.

"Nothing. Never mind."

Detective Ford shrugged. "Suit yourself." He clicked on the car radio just in time to hear the radio announcer report that the NAACP and several other civil rights organizations were planning protests in Toby county.

Ford and Bailey exchanged surprised glances. The town of Saint Molasses didn't have their own local radio station. Most of the radio programming were from nearby cities. They hadn't realized that their small town had made national headlines.

Bailey turned up the volume.

"Martin Luther King Jr must be turning in his grave right now! Why are these coloreds so angry? We should be the ones angry! They're the ones slaughtering and kidnapping whites in that godforsaken town! Why is the NAACP involving themselves with these criminals anyway?"

"Great." Ford muttered. "Last thing we need is to worry about protests." He said, reflecting on the L.A. Watts riot that had made national headlines just four years ago.

"I don't get it." Bailey said. "Why are the negros so upset?"

As if the radio host had heard the detective's inquiry, he stated, *"Several colored organizations are stating that the negroes being arrested in Saint Molasses, are not being granted a lawyer or a fair trial. Ladies and gentlemen, what else is there to determine? These animals are killing and kidnapping hardworking Americans! Mothers! Daughters! Sons! I say give them all the death penalty!"*

"I reckon it's gonna be a loooong night." Ford groaned, pulling up to the sheriff's office. "Deputy Aiken's got a nigger in there been beggin' and hollerin' to speak to us."

Bailey furrowed his brow. "He wants to talk to us? Who is he?"

"Just one 'em coloreds that got arrested." He answered, parking.

The two men entered the police department and were led to a small room with a long table, where a bald colored man in handcuffs sat waiting. He stood as soon as the detectives entered.

"Dylan! Ed!" The man shouted. "You gotta help me!"

"Sit down!" Ford ordered. He walked over to the long table and narrowed his eyes at the man. "You *will* refer to us Detective Ford and Detective Bailey, you understand?"

"But Dylan, you don't understand." The man said, still standing.

"Sit your ass down." Ford growled. He waited until the man was seated, before he sat across from him.

"What is it you needed to tell us?" Bailey asked, sitting beside Ford.

"It's me." The man said, his voice breaking. "It's Barney."

The two detectives looked at one another.

"Barney who?" Ford asked.

"Barney Harper." The colored man stared at Bailey with pleading eyes. "Ed, it's me. Your neighbor."

"Barney Harper?" Ford snickered. "You 'spect us to believe you live over on the north side with the middle-class whites, boy?"

Bailey shook his head at the man. "Even if you did live on the north side, I ain't never seen you over yonder. Matter of fact, I never seen you once ever in Molasses. 'Til now, that is."

"Where ya really from?" Ford asked. "'And who's your leader? Why are you people kidnapping our residents?"

The man, ignoring Ford, stared at Bailey. "My wife is Shannon Harper. We have two daughters, Trudy and Carol Harper. I have a son Lee Harper, who everyone 'round town calls Boo Harper. He lives over in those trailers at Meadowbrook Square with his mom, Edith."

"Wait, how did you-" Bailey began.

He was quickly interrupted by the colored man. "Last fall, I let you hold my leaf blower and you still haven't returned the sonofabitch. Yer wife, Shelby, makes the best apple strudel pie in town. My oldest daughter, Carol, walks to the high school with yer daughter, Abigail, every morning."

"Now hold on just a doggone minute!" Ford hollered. He stood to his feet and grabbed the suspect by his striped jumpsuit. "Are you threatening my partner over here? Have you and yer nigger friends been spyin' on the Baileys and the Harpers?"

Bailey, shaken by the accurate information, glared at the suspect. "If anyone so much as lay a finger on our family, I will *kill* you." He threatened. "You hear me? I will lock you back in this room and kill you. You hear me?"

"I'll be right back, Bailey." Ford announced. "I'm gonna go see Sheriff Woods about having yer house and the Harper's property under twenty-four-hour police surveillance immediately."

"Thank you, Ford." Bailey said. He vowed to himself to buy his daughter, Abigail, an automobile to get to and from school. It was no longer safe for the two girls to walk alone.

"Ed." Barney said, tentatively.

"What the fuck have I ever done to you?" Bailey asked. "I don't bother you people. Sure, I sometimes look the other way when my partner.....*handle* you people, but why should I suffer? I'm not a racist."

"Ed. Close your eyes and just listen to me. Please." He pleaded. *"Please."*

Reluctantly, Detective Bailey did as he was told.

"Ed. It's me, Barney Harper, your neighbor of over twenty years. I don't know what happened. I don't know how this happen, but yesterday morning I woke up to Shannon screaming right in my ear. I git' right up and she starts throwing stuff at me: lamps, shoes, pillows, anything else she can get her hands on."

Bailey opened his eyes as Barney continued.

"I ask her what's wrong and she's not answering. Alls she doing is calling me a nigger." Barney said, wiping the tears forming in his eyes.

Bailey stared at the man. He couldn't deny the fact that the man favored his neighbor, but the story didn't make sense. It was physically and scientifically impossible unless... "You ever heard 'bout that white Texan journalist who took pills or whatnot to change the color of his skin?" Bailey asked.

Barney shook his head. "Don't think I have."

Detective Bailey nodded. "His name is John Howard Griffin. Did it to see what it felt like to be a negro. Wrote a book about it and all."

"And you say he took pills?" Barney asked, slightly relieved that the detective seemed to believe him.

"I think it was pills or drops. Point is, there's probably a reasonable explanation for this. If you're who you say you are."

"Ed, me being who I say I am is the least of your problems."

Bailey raised a brow. "What do ya mean?"

Barney sighed. "See, there's a lot of colored folks locked up in the county jail who used to be white like you."

Bailey slowly furrowed his brows in confusion.

Barney continued. "And as far as I see, it's gonna keep happenin'. Pretty soon, there won't be anymore room at the county jail to hol' all of us. Ed, you need to get the CIA and the FBI on this. This is much bigger than Saint Molasses. Much bigger than this small-town law enforcement office."

"If what you're saying is true, who or what do you think is behind this?" Bailey asked, retrieving his pen and pad.

"I don't know. At first I thought it might've been the coloreds on the south side."

Bailey looked up from his notepad. "And now?"

"Not sure. You've got no idea what it's like to be a negro, Ed. Guards and everyone else, including the other white inmates, treat me like I'm lower than cow's dung. Did you know, they give the colored and white inmates different meals. Been eating spoiled potted meat and vegetables since I been in here."

Bailey wasn't going to admit that he already knew about the spoiled meals for negroes.

"Believe it or not," Barney continued, staring at his fingers. "Some of the coloreds in there, the *real* coloreds, they aren't that bad. Some of 'em locked up in there when they ought not to be. Arrested for the silliest made-up infractions. They took me right in as their own when they seen me. Shared some of their stuff with me and whatnot.

Ain't too bad, them coloreds." He looked up at Bailey. "Would it be too much to ask of you to git' me a copy of that book by the Griffin fella?"

"I'll see what I can do." Bailey answered, surprising himself.

BLACK · OUT ·

CHAPTER
FIFTEEN

"Wedon't rent out rooms to niggers. Can't you read?" Renee Thatcher repeated snidely, pointing at the sign on the door that read, *No Niggers Allowed.* She twisted her mouth into a severe scowl as she eyed the negro woman from head to toe. The galls of this woman to use the front door, instead of the side door like all the other coloreds.

"*Please?*" The woman pleaded. "Just for the night? I don't mind payin' extra."

Renee turned up her nose in disgust. She couldn't stand uppity niggers. She eyed the woman's expensive sandals, yellow dress, and her ridiculous large blonde afro. "You hard of hearin' or somethin'? We don't want yer money."

The colored woman took in a deep breath as she collected herself. She knew if Renee Thatcher knew who she really was, she'd be kissing her ass from here to Marmalade. "Fine. I'll take my money somewhere else then."

Renne stared at the woman's blue eyes pensively. "You wouldn't happen to be kin to that nigger with the blue eyes who killed the Haynes, would ya?"

Georgia gasped. "No! *God, no!*"

"You's both got the same blue eyes. Must be kin." Renee accused.

"No. I'm Georgia Daniels. Well, Georgia Murphy, now." She corrected, preferring to go by her maiden name. She dug into her purse and placed her identification on the counter. "See? It's me, Georgia."

The clerk dragged the I.D. with her ink pen, as if the item were contaminated. She looked at the I.D., then back up at the colored woman. "Whatchu' doin' with Mrs. Daniels' identification?" She asked. She wasn't exactly friends with the Daniels, but everyone knew who they were. The Daniels were one of the most attractive middle-class folks with the best teeth in town. They lived across town, on the other side of Meadowbrook, the trailer park Renee resided in. If it weren't for the fact that she detested that snooty Marilyn Monroe wanna-be, she would've kept the identification for safekeeping and phoned the police.

"No, you don't understand." Georgia said desperately "Look, it's *me*. When I woke up this morning-"

"Do I look like I care?" Renee interjected. "If I were you, I'd leave 'fore I get a good mind to ring the sheriff's office."

"The sheriff's office? But I haven't done a thing!"

Renee picked up the rotary phone and began dialing.

"Alright, alright. There's no need to call the law. I'm leaving." Georgia said in defeat. She held her head down in shame as she grabbed her luggage.

Georgia walked two miles in the sweltering heat, before sitting at an empty bus stop. She cried and cursed when she heard the low rumble of thunder.

She hadn't been sitting for two minutes when a white man inside a red Oldsmobile, crawled to a stop in front of her.

She recognized the man as Pastor Buddy Peabody, the assistant church pastor of the only church in Saint Molasses. He waved her over to his Oldsmobile.

Georgia breathed a sigh of relief. Finally, someone had come to her rescue. She grabbed her luggage, slung it onto the backseat of the car, and climbed into the passenger side.

"Thank you so much, Pastor." Georgia said sincerely.

"Oh, it's not a problem." He replied, pulling away from the curb.

"I mean it." Georgia said. "You don't know what kind of a day I've had."

"Glad I could help." He replied, resting his hand on her thighs.

Georgia looked ahead uneasily. "If you could drop me off at one of the colored inns in Marmalade, I'd be grateful."

"I'll see what I can do, pretty lady." He winked.

"Thank you, pastor."

"You're more than welcome to sleep over at our place for the night." He offered.

Georgia smiled as she declined. "Oh no, I wouldn't feel right inconveniencing you and Mrs. Peabody."

"Mrs. Peabody's away at her sister's for the next coupla days. I insist. Just for the night. Nothin' wrong with savin' yerself a little money." He said, placing his big hairy hands back on top of her thighs.

"No thank you, pastor. Matter of fact, you can just drop me off here."

Pastor Peabody remained silent as he pulled into a wooded area.

"Where we goin'?"

He stopped the vehicle in the middle of the woods and turned off the ignition.

"Pastor Peabody?"

His large paws travelled over her long yellow dress, up to her bosoms. "I've always loved you negro girls." He panted.

Georgia's mouth opened in astonishment as the assistant pastor continued to grope her.

"Get your hands off of me!" She shrieked, attempting to pry his large hands off of her chest.

"Come 'ere nigger." He growled. He opened his side of the door and held on to her arm, pulling her out of the Oldsmobile behind him.

"Let go of me!"

Buddy Peabody used one hand to unzip his slacks as he leaned his full weight onto Georgia, who was pressed against the automobile.

"Get off of me!" She cried, clawing away at his arms and face. "*Heeeelp!*"

"Ow!" He yelped in agitation as he felt his face for blood. Sure enough, he was bleeding on the right side of his face. He reared his hand back and slapped her before tossing her on the grass.

Georgia cried in relief as she watched him open the door to the driver's side of the vehicle.

"Wait! My luggage!" She yelled, springing to her feet. She swiftly opened the back door of the Oldsmobile. The door hadn't been open for more than five seconds, before he drove off. Luckily for Georgia, she was able to pull out her luggage before he took off.

"You dirty old nasty man!" She shouted at the Oldsmobile, before breaking down into tears.

She headed back to the main road, when it began to pour.

"Doggone it!" She cried out, carrying her luggage over her blonde afro. "I just can't catch a break!"

CHAPTER
SIXTEEN

The first twenty-four hours after the children had been gracious enough to feed Rusty and provide him a change of clothing, both his hands had returned to its normal pigment. Noah and Ida still felt conflicted on whether he should call the authorities or let the boy go.

"I gotta head to work soon." He told Ida and Malcolm during breakfast. "Keep an eye on *the package*." He instructed them.

Malcolm nodded.

"What package?" Savannah asked Noah curiously, as she took a seat between Marley and Charlene.

Ida quickly interjected. "Did they ever find that ol' white lady you worked for?" She asked Charlene, in an attempt to change the subject.

"Not yet. As much as I couldn't stand working for that old wench, I'm still worried about 'er. She had no family. Lord knows where she could be."

"What about the old lady they found lynched in her bedroom?" Malcolm asked.

"Lynched?" Savannah frowned. "It was ruled a suicide, Malcolm."

"You should know better than to trust anything The Man says." Malcolm countered. "Why would a colored woman break in a honky's home, just to commit suicide? Just not addin' up."

"Did the old colored woman look like Mrs. Browne?" Ida asked curiously.

Malcolm and Noah glanced at one another.

"Hunh?" Charlene replied, confused.

"Savannah," Mrs. McGwire called out, walking in the small dining area adjacent to the even tinier kitchen. "Has Noah left for work already?"

"I'm right here, mama." Noah answered, mouth full of porridge.

"You make sure you come right home after work, you hear?" Mrs. McGwire instructed, smoothing out her bright white uniform, the very one that the Wiggins insisted she wear when tending to their three messy children.

Noah frowned. "Me and a few other guys are planning to meet up at Malik's after work. It'll take me at least twenty minutes just to walk over there."

Mrs. McGwire folded her arms as she stared at her eldest son. "I don't care what you had planned after work, I need you to be home immediately after work. I wish you all would quit callin' him Malik. His mama named him Leroy Johnson."

Savannah and Charlene snickered.

"Malik Abdullah's his Islamic name, mama." Noah explained.

Mrs. McGwire placed a hand on her hip. "I don't want you getting caught up with that militant. All he does is bring attention to hisself with his 'revolution' talk." She looked around the table at her other children. "I don't want anyone outside after four, ya hear me?"

"But mama," Savannah protested.

"But mama, nothin'.'" Mrs. McGwire snapped. "The south side of town is still under curfew. Didn't y'all hear what happened to Anthony Taylor last night?"

"You mean Asaad Shakur?" Savannah smirked. "He done converted to Islam too, mama."

Mrs. McGwire frowned. "Whatever it is he go by now. Point is, they beat 'em almost half to death for sassin' off 'fore lockin' him up for breakin' curfew. Like I said before, I don't want any of you out after four. Especially you, Noah, or have you also converted?"

"But mama," Charlene groaned. "They only targeting members of Malik's militant group. Why do we all gotta suffer on account of Noah and his silly friends?"

"How could you call my friends silly when we're trying more than anyone to make changes for negros in Molasses?" Noah asked. "Sitting indoors and acceptin' this way of life ain't bringin' 'bout no change."

Savannah nodded. "Those pigs have always had a problem with Anthony-uh-Asaad on account of that civil rights stuff he's always preachin'."

"You sho' is right, Savannah." Mrs. McGwire agreed. She turned to Noah. "You stay away from those boys, you hear?"

"What? Come on, mama." Noah protested, then scowled at his eldest sister from across the small table.

"Ma," Ida called out. "Curfew is six o'clock. Why do we have to be in so early?"

Mrs. McGwire walked over to Ida. "I don't care what the town's curfew is. Long as you're living under this roof, your curfew is four. Everyone is to be home at four o'clock sharp. Is that understood?" She asked all six of the McGwire children.

"*Yes, mama.*" They all replied in unison.

Acknowledging the collective looks of disappointment around the dining table, she said, "Now I'm not happy 'bout this curfew either, but there's been more police cars 'round here patrolling than ever before. Some of 'em is just itchin' for a reason to be bothersome to coloreds. 'Specially since that Haynes murderer still out loose."

Noah, Ida, and Malcolm looked at one another.

"I don't know why they're over here harrassin' us." Savannah pouted. "They should be over on the north side and Meadowbrook Square patrolling. That's where all the break-ins are happenin'."

Malcolm snickered.

"What's so funny?" Savannah snapped.

Malcolm shook his head. "Since when have these honkies ever needed a reason to dictate our lives?"

Charlene nodded. "Can't believe I'm sayin' this but Malcolm has a point. They treat all us colored folks like chil'ren. I ain't the least bit surprised 'bout this curfew. It's like we're all simpletons with them chaperoning us, and whatnot. Bad enough they dictate where and how we live. Did you know Janet Foster's dad been workin' over at the white school as a janitor for over twenty year and ain't seen a nary raise the whole time he been breakin' his back cleanin' their nasty toilets and whatnot?"

"The NAACP's fixin' to come to Molasses. Hopefully, it'll help change some thangs 'round here." Mrs. McGwire informed.

Ida chimed in. "Luanne Stuart told me at school the other day that her pa told her that the FBI was also fixin' to come here, on account of the Haynes killer."

"Where were they when these white folks were huntin' and lynching us like fish couple months ago?" Malcolm asked angrily. "Funny how soon as white folks are bein' kidnapped and murdered, it's a national concern. I hope the Haynes killer git' all of em!"

Mrs. McGwire placed a hand on Malcolm's shoulder. "Now, Malcolm, I understand why you're upset, but wrong is wrong. Taking another's life is a downright sin. What you think Jesus would say hearin' you talk like that?"

Malcolm frowned. "That's the white man's religion, mama."

Ida both groaned, knowing where this was going. "You're starting to sound just like Malik and his militant group."

"Well they might be on to somethin', then." Malcolm admitted.

Mrs. McGwire gave him a stern look. "Malcolm, yer daddy and I done already told you to keep your religious beliefs out this house. We don't need Marley and Ida here being influenced. This here's a Christian household. You hear me?"

Malcolm lowered his eyes. "Yes, ma'am."

She looked over at Noah. "Ain't it 'bout time for you to git' goin'? These bills ain't gonna pay itself."

Noah nodded before downing the rest of his orange juice. "Now you remember what I said."

Again, Noah nodded. "Come straight home after work. I got it." He looked over at Malcolm, then at Ida. "Don't forget." He said, pointing his chin in the direction of the shed.

Ida nodded. "Yeah. *The package.* We know."

Savannah looked at Marley curiously. "Have any idea what they're talkin' 'bout?" She whispered.

Marley hesitated before answering. "Noah and Malcolm made me promise not to tell." He whispered back.

Savannah nodded. "I got a Bazooka and a Lemonhead with your name on it if you let me in on y'all little secret. How's that sound?"

His eyes lit up. He grinned, then peeked around the table at his siblings, who were already on to the next topic. "Deal."

BLACK · OUT ·

CHAPTER
SEVENTEEN

Jimmy stirred from his sleep on the living room sofa the next morning. He hadn't even remembered falling asleep. Last thing he remembered was watching the Mayor's press conference late last night, while waiting for Georgia to come back home.

Hearing shouts and cries outside, he immediately sat up. "What in the world is going on out there?"

He made his way to the window and slid the curtains over. His brows raised at the sight of three police cars parked across the street, in front of the neighbor's home. His neighbor, Sheila Devereaux, was being comforted by a female deputy. He watched as a male officer escorted a pudgy colored man with an extremely voluminous afro, out the home in handcuffs. The man's mouth opened and closed as he shouted.

Eager to hear what the man had to say, Jimmy opened his door and stepped outside. He spotted other neighbors peeking from their curtains and some even spectating in plain sight, as he was now doing.

"I *am* Jon Devereaux!" The man said. "I live here! Why are you arresting me! I've done nothing! Sheila, tell them!"

"I don't know him!" Mrs. Devereaux shouted back angrily. "Ask him what he's done with my husband! Jon-Jon's missing!"

Jimmy and a few other neighbors walked over to the Devereaux residence.

"It's me, Sheila!" The man shouted, struggling to get out the grasps of officers.

"Hey!" One officer shouted. "Knock it off!"

"I want an attorney!" The man demanded. "I have a right to an attorney! I am gonna sue the britches off of Saint Molasses!"

Another officer walked over to the suspect and kneed the cuffed man in the groin, causing him to crumple to the ground in anguish. Neighbors rooted as two other officers began attacking the middle-aged colored man on the ground.

Jimmy cringed.

"I just want my husband! Someone, please, find Jon-Jon!" Mrs. Devereaux cried out.

Trembling, Jimmy sprinted back inside his home just as a news van had arrived.

"How's it goin', Jimmy?"

Jimmy nearly fainted at the sight of the young man he'd met at the drug store, sitting on his couch like he'd been there the whole time. He had on the same black cap with the large white X.

"How'd you get in here?" He asked, still standing cautiously at his door. He eyed the boy's oversized jeans and thought it was strange for him to be wearing a basketball jersey over a white t-shirt.

"Shut the door, Jimmy. We need to talk."

Jimmy did as he was told. He slowly walked towards the armchair and sat across from him. "Who are you?"

"My name is Frederick King, but you can call me Freddie."

"Why are you here and-and how'd you disappear that night? I seen you disappear. Where did you come from?"

83

Freddie held up both his hands. "Hold on. You're talkin' too fast, man. I told you before: I'm from Negus." Freddie noticed the look of curiosity on Jimmy's face as he stared at Freddie's sneakers. "You like 'em?" He asked, bending down to dust off his shoes. "These are Jordans. They don't come out for another three decades or so."

"I asked several of the guys at the firm if they've ever heard of ...Negus. Not a single one of 'em had heard of it."

"No one around here would know about Negus." Freddie explained.

"Well, I checked the Encyclopedia Britannica at work. Couldn't find nothin'. Now how do ya' explain that? "

"I told you when we first met. You wouldn't have heard of Negus. It's in a whole different solar system, Jimmy."

"So... would that technically classify you as an alien?"

Freddie chuckled. "My sister was right about you guys. Y'all sure do love classifying and compartmentalizing everything. Ever care to think that maybe we're all just one with the universe?"

Convinced that the boy had to be on some type of acid, he stood to his feet as he asked, "Did you have anything to do with the disappearance of Margaret Brown? Better yet, are you the Haynes murderer?"

"Ahh, the Haynes. What a tragedy."

"Did you kill 'em?" Jimmy repeated. If he admitted to it, he figured he'd run outside and get the law.

"Rusty Jr. killed his parents. Killed them in an act of self-defense."

"Do you know where he is? Is he dead?" He asked, sitting back down.

"Oh, he's alive. Don't quite look the same, though."

"What do you mean?"

"Is the wife home?" Freddie asked.

Jimmy furrowed his brow. "N-no. No, she's not. Wait, how did you-?"

"You did the right thing you know. Telling her the truth."

Jimmy lowered his head as he sighed.

"It's who you are, Jimmy. There's no changing that."

"It's not that simple. You wouldn't understand."

"Think so?"

Jimmy's eyes lit up. "Are you able to fix her?"

"Who?"

"Georgia. My wife. Her skin's-"

"What for?" Freddie interjected. "If I changed her now, it won't bring her back to you."

"So how-?"

"She is the only person who can fix herself. Starts with the inside." He said, standing up to leave.

"Where you going?" Jimmy asked, also standing. "What about everyone else? You can't just leave everyone like this. Not without an explanation."

Freddie chuckled. "What do you expect me to do? Hold a press conference?"

"I don't know. I expect you to do something. Anything!" He pleaded, thinking of how unfair this was for Mr. and Mrs. Devereaux and all the others.

This time there was no mistaking that Freddie's eyes were flickering from brown to blue, as he looked to be in deep thought. "Don't worry. Pretty soon majority of the town will transform. Well, not everyone. People like you are excluded."

"Like me?" Jimmy repeated, placing a hand on his chest.

Freddie simply nodded, not bothering to elaborate.

Jimmy stared helplessly at him. "They're locking innocent people up."

"Don't worry. It's all temporary. They'll eventually change back, if they change on the inside."

"And if they don't?" Jimmy asked. "People are dying. They just found Renee Thatcher dead in her boyfriend's apartment. He shot her, thinking she was an intruder."

"There's no such thing as death, but we can discuss that at another time. Eventually the whole town, with an exception of a few kind people, will wake up as people of color. There's nothing that can be done about it. They are killing irrationally in an act of ignorance and fear." His eyes flickered blue again, as he appeared to be staring into the distance. "This will force the release of all innocently jailed. Including those wrongly convicted before the phenomena."

Jimmy stared at him skeptically. "How do you know?"

Freddie tapped the middle of his forehead with his index finger. "Let's just say I got a pretty sharp third-eye."

CHAPTER
EIGHTEEN

"I still can't wrap my mind around it." Earline said, shaking her head.

Sitting across from Earline at her small kitchen table, Penny Thorton looked downright spooked. "First Shirley and now Renee? Shirley is one of the toughest old biddies in Molasses. If she weren't able to fight 'em off, ain't no hope for the rest of us." This had hit too close to home for Penny. Shirley Dalton had just organized the neighborhood watch a few days ago. The tight-knit trailer community still could not figure out how the kidnapper had gotten past Augustus, Billy Jean, and Horace, who had all been out on watch that night.

Penny watched as Earline pulled in the toxins from her Parliament Light. She wanted to remind Earline that she was pregnant, but was too afraid. Like Shirley, Earline was just as downright intimidating.

"Like I told y'all before," Earline said, "I dare one of them niggers to break in my trailer. Got a bullet just waitin' on 'em."

Penny thought about the Dobermann her live-in boy-friend, Raymond, had talked about purchasing. She reflected on how Shirley had warned her that a dog wasn't gonna stop an intruder with a gun. "I think I'm gonna ask Ray to get us a gun. Either that or move to another trailer park in Marma-lade."

Earline cackled, eyeing Penny with a look of pity. "You really gonna let them spooks run you from your own town? I have a rifle I can spare ya." Earline offered. "It's Dylan's, but he won't even notice it's gone. 'Long as you return it 'fore huntin' season."

Penny nodded. "I appreciate that." She was almost tempted to ask Earline for a cigarette. Her nerves had gotten so bad, that every thump and creak she heard caused her to jump.

"Got anymore Cola?" Earline asked, rubbing her belly. "This little one's craving some more Cola."

Penny stood to her feet to grab two RC Colas from the refrigerator. "Heard the NAACP is fixin' to have a protest in Molasses." She informed, placing a long-neck bottle in front of Earline.

"Who gives a hoot? I'm downright sick of talkin' 'bout this. Everywhere I go, everywhere I look, they're either talkin' 'bout this or the Vietnam war. Let's talk about somethin' else, *please*." Earline vented.

"That's fine with me." Penny agreed, tired of feeling anxious every waking moment.

"Did you catch Bonanza yesterday?" Earline asked.

"No. Yesterday I finally got Ray to watch *Julia* with me. Forgot all about Bonanza. Was it good?"

Earline twisted her mouth into a scowl. "Julia?"

"You know, that show with Diahann Carroll?"

"If I didn't know any better, I'd swear you were a nigger-lover." Earline hissed.

Penny's jaws clenched. "I am not a—a—I am *not* one of those." Penny stammered. She could never bring herself to use the word 'nigger'. She had been raised to respect coloreds as equals.

"I gotta get going." Earline announced, sliding her seat away from the circular table.

Penny couldn't help noticing the disgusted look on her neighbor's face. "You okay?" She asked, rising to her feet.

Earline scowled. "I can't fraternize or whatnot with a nigger-lover, Penny. I just can't do it." She repeated, tempted to remind Penny that Dylan was a respected member of the klan.

Penny grabbed Earline's arm. "I promise you, Earline. I am not a...uh..negro lover."

CHAPTER
NINETEEN

"It's over this way." Marley said, leading Savannah by the hand.

Savannah scrunched her nose. "Outside? Won't you just tell me what it is?"

"Almost there."

Realizing they were headed to the shed, Savannah asked, "Is it a bike or somethin'? What is it, Marley?"

"Lemme show you."

"Marlon James McGwire! What do ya' think you're doin?" Ida called out a few feet behind them. Marley and Savannah were both startled.

"She promised me Bazooka gum and Lemonheads." Marley admitted ashamedly.

"Savannah, you shouldn't go in there." Ida said, drawing near them.

Savannah placed a hand on her hip and narrowed her eyes at Ida. "What's the big problem? Why can't I go in there?"

"Because," Ida began. "Because...uh.." She looked around as she tried to think.

"Because we know how much you're afraid of spiders." Malcolm quickly replied, walking up behind them.

Savannah eyes widened. "Spiders?" She glanced from Marley to Malcolm, then took a few steps back.

"Yes." Ida confirmed. "We growin' a tarantula farm."

"A tarantula farm?" Savannah repeated, squirming as if she could feel them crawling all over her thin body. "I'm gonna tell mama."

"You do that and I'll hide one in you drawer." Ida threatened.

Savannah glowered at her. "You guys had better get rid of 'em before the weekend or I'm tellin'." She threatened before stomping off in the other direction.

Malcolm and Ida frowned at Marley.

"She promised me Bazooka and Lemonhead."

Malcolm shook a fist at his brother. "Well I'm promising you a knuckle sandwich if you open that mouth again."

The three McGwire children entered the flimsy shed. Rusty was still chained and curled in a ball on top of a pallet as he slept.

Ida reached inside her shirt and pulled out a ham sandwich. She kicked the sleeping boy's feet. "Git up! Time for breakfast."

Rusty slowly sat up, wiping the sleep from his eyes. He reached for the sandwich. "Thank you, Ida."

Malcolm retrieved a pair of clean underwear from his back pocket. He threw them in front of Rusty, still careful about catching whatever skin-changing disease the boy had. "Here ya go, man."

"Thanks, Malcolm."

"I've got a special surprise for you, Rusty." Marley informed.

He knelt beside Rusty and pulled out an individually wrapped Bazooka and two Lemonheads from the front pocket of his corduroy overalls.

"Here." He offered, placing one Lemonhead in front of Rusty. He then unwrapped the Bazooka and stretched the piece of gum until it was split in half.

Rusty, just a kid himself, nearly cried. "Thank you, Marley."

Malcolm tried to hide his smile. "Ida, you stay here with Marley and Rusty. I'll get him somethin' to wash that sandwich down with."

It had been several days since the children had all discussed whether or not they should release their hostage. Ida was still adamant that they should let him go. Malcolm had initially wanted to turn him in, as some act of revenge against whites. After spending so much time with Rusty Jr., he was now undecided. Noah was also on the fence, although he often thought about the reward money. His conscience did not sit well with knowing that an innocent person would be executed on account of him. They were all aware that as soon as the law had their hands on him, he would be charged with the murders and all the kidnappings in Molasses. He would for sure receive capital punishment. To Rusty's own surprise, he no longer wanted to be released. Saint Molasses seemed like such a cold and scary world to him now that he was colored. Since that fateful morning when he had been left to survive on his own, this had been the first time he hadn't had to worry about where to sleep, find food, bathing, or simply having companionship. He didn't mind staying in there with the creepy crawly spiders and rodents. He was just happy to be safe and alive.

Malcolm headed towards the entrance of the shed. "Ida, lock the door behind me. We don't need Savannah or anyone else snoopin' 'round here, seeing what we're really up to."

Ida did as she was told before rejoining Rusty and Marley.

"Could you at least unchain me?" Rusty asked her. "I'm not goin' anywhere. I have nowhere to go."

"What about your sister, Julia, from California? The news been reporting that she's supposed to be coming back to town any day now. They aren't sayin' 'xactly which day on account of the Haynes murderer. They don't want her to be a target." Ida said.

"Well that's just silly. There ain't no real Haynes murderer. They make it seem as if there's some psycho killer runnin' 'round Molasses." He said.

Ida nodded. "And guess who those white folks and The Man got their eyes set on, now."

"Who?" Marley asked.

"Mind your manners, Marley." Ida chastised. "This is grown folk talk." She looked back at Rusty. "This whole fiasco has gotten everyone keepin' a close eye at coloreds on the south side. Mama said she was riding the bus to work when all of a sudden the bus stopped and a whole bunch of police officers got on to check every colored person for weapons."

"I'm not ready to go out there." Rusty said nervously.

"Look atcha'. Afraid to walk the life of a negro. This is the life we got to live every day, Rusty. We ain't got no say in it and we don't have the option of hiding from the world."

Rusty sat quiet, letting Ida ramble on as he thought about what she had just said.

CHAPTER
TWENTY

A*in't this just dandy?* Georgia thought.

After being left stranded by Buddy Peabody, she continued walking on the side of the road in the rain for the next two miles, too afraid to hitch hike again. It wasn't until the rain had settled down some, did she realize that she was less than ten yards away from the Wakefield's residence.

"Thank heavens!" Georgia praised, trying her best to run in her designer kitten heels toward the Wakefield's.

Georgia rang the doorbell of the lavish country-style home just as it began thundering.

"Oh c'mon. C'mon, answer the door." She whispered impatiently.

"What do you want?" Her best friend, Eugenia Wakefield, barked coldly behind a locked screen door, aiming a rifle at Georgia.

"Eugenia. Boy am I happy to see you." Georgia cried.

Eugenia peered at the colored woman. "I thought my husband told you, we didn't want you coming in to work until the Hayne's murderers were caught, Millie."

"Millie?" Georgia repeated. "No, it's me. Georgia."

"This some kinda' joke? Get off my porch 'fore my husband come home. Else you'll really be sorry."

Georgia's throat tightened. "Eugenia, it's *me*."

"You's got three seconds to git' off my property, darkie."

"Darkie?"

"Now!"

"This is gonna sound really crazy right now, Eugenia,-"

"One." Eugenia began counting.

"Can't I just come in for a minute and explain-"

"Two." She continued, aiming at Georgia.

"If you'd just listen to what I'm trying to tell-"

Both Georgia and Eugenia were startled by the deafening blast of the rifle. The leaves of a large potted fern behind Georgia rustled.

Stunned Georgia looked at her best friend. "You almost shot me!"

"Git' offa' my property, nigger! Git or I won't miss next time!" She warned, aiming straight at her chest.

Without another word, Georgia picked up her suitcase and scattered off the porch, into the pouring rain.

Georgia was back on the lone wet highway and after a few hours, not only had she grown tired, but she was famished.

"Hey!" Georgia heard a woman's voice call out.

She stopped walking and looked over to find a young colored woman inside a brown Plymouth Fury smiling at her.

"Need a lift?" The young woman asked.

Georgia hesitated. "But I'm all wet." She said, looking down at her drenched yellow dress.

"Girl, it's fine. Get in. Not a wise idea for a colored woman to be out after curfew."

Georgia stood still, unsure of what she should do. She wasn't sure if the woman was a negro resident of Saint Molasses. They all looked alike to her.

"Besides, you look hungry and I gotta a few snacks in here." The woman held up a red apple and a bottle of water

Eying the snacks hungrily, Georgia grabbed her luggage and climbed into the Plymouth.

"I'm Rosa King." The woman greeted as soon as Georgia had shut the door. "You are?"

"Georgia. Georgia Dan-Murphy."

"Where ya headed?" Rosa asked, pulling off.

"Marmalade." Georgia answered, biting into the apple.

"Looks like you're in luck. Headed that way myself."

Georgia looked over at her suspiciously. "I don't think I've ever seen you in Molasses before."

"I don't come over to the wealthy side of town often. Heard the law love harassing us colored over on this side." Rosa answered. "What are ya doin' on this side of town anyway?"

Georgia sniffled, attempting to stop her tears from flowing. "I just wanted to find a room to sleep in tonight. Been walkin' damn near the whole doggone day."

"Aww, don't cry, darlin'. You can stay with my brother and I 'til you get yourself situated."

"Oh, I couldn't." Georgia sniffled.

"Well, where else you gonna go? You have family 'round here?"

Georgia shook her head. This time, she allowed herself to sob. The one person, other than her husband, that she had considered family had run her off her front porch with a shot gun. "They're all in South Carolina."

Rosa patted her arm . "Well, then, you can stay with us." She looked at the blonde tangled afro sitting awry on top of her head. "We'll do somethin' with that beautiful hair of yours, too."

Pulling up to an inn in Marmalade, Georgia never thought she'd feel so indebted to a negro as she did that evening.

Rosa helped the woman grab her luggage before the two women headed inside.

"Freddie!" Rosa called out as soon as they had entered.

"He's not here. He's still over in Molasses." A woman's voice shouted from inside the bathroom.

"Come on out, Zee, I got somebody I want you to meet." Rosa looked over at Georgia, who still looked shaken up. She laughed before telling her, "You look like a scared puppy. Have a seat, girl. We won't bite. Better yet you can shower and change first, if you'd like."

A hot shower is exactly what Georgia thought she needed. "Thanks." She smiled awkwardly at the woman.

The bathroom door clicked open and out walked a gorgeous young woman the color of fudge in a bright yellow swimsuit. She had her hair braided in the tiniest cornrows.

"Zee, I want you to meet Georgia. I found her walking on the side of the road in Molasses after curfew."

The woman extended a hand to Georgia, accompanied with a warm smile. "How ya' doin' sista'?"

"Georgia, this is Zora Newton. She's my brother's girlfriend."

"You can call me Zee." Zora offered.

"Nice to make your acquaintance....Zee."

"You have an awful lot of hair, girl." Zora noted, staring at the woman's blonde hair in awe.

Rosa nodded in agreement. "I told her we'd hook her up."

"Well I was just about to head downstairs for a swim. Y'all coming?" Zora asked.

"Count me in." Rosa said.

Georgia crinkled her nose at the thought of sharing the same body of water as coloreds. "I really just wanna shower and rest a little. Y'all go on without me."

"Might wanna go on ahead and wash your hair while you're at it." Rosa suggested. "Zora and I will help get those knots out soon as we get back."

"That sounds just dandy. Thank you." Georgia replied.

Rosa suddenly frowned at Zora. "Zee, is that my bathing suit?"

Zora smiled impishly. Placing her hand on her head, she struck a pose. "It's cute on me. Don't ya' think?"

Rosa chuckled. "Well, what am I supposed to wear, Zee?"

"You can wear mine."

Georgia made her way to the bathroom, then cringed when she remembered that she hadn't packed a towel. She stuck her head out the bathroom door and called out to Rosa.

"What's the matter, darlin'?" Rosa asked, walking towards the bathroom.

"Do you mind running downstairs and asking for a clean towel? I left mine at home."

Rosa furrowed her brows. "There aren't any more in there?"

Georgia smiled weakly at the younger woman. "I'd rather just have a freshly washed towel, please."

"Sure, anything else?"

"Uhh-yes. I'll also need a fresh bar of soap, a toothbrush, toothpaste, and a bottle of Clorox."

"Clorox?" Rosa queried.

Georgia smiled weakly. "Yeah. I-uh- got a phobia of-uh-germs and whatnot on account of my aunt Sandy dying of a severe case of Malaria two years ago." She lied.

"I'm sorry to hear that. I'll be right back with everything." Rosa assured.

Oh fudge, I forgot to ask her to bring me a bottle of shampoo. A few minutes later, Rosa handed her all of the requested items, including a miniature bottle of shampoo. Georgia prayed that the bleach would protect her from any colored diseases her mother had always warned her about growing up.

"Well I'll be damned." Georgia said, once she was done showering. She stared at her washed mane in the dingy mirror. She was surprised to find that her thick coiled hair no longer sat straight up on her head. Instead, her blonde hair dripped with water as it lay and hung below her shoulders. She grabbed a strand and studied how the tight springy coils were now loose and relaxed when wet. "I reckon this is kinda.... *groovy.*"

Georgia wrapped her nude slender body with the towel Rosa had provided. She was in the middle of rummaging through her suitcase for something to sleep in, when streams of red and blue dancing lights peeked through the motel's vertical blinds. With her body still wrapped in the inn's towel, she trotted to the window and found a Marmalade police vehicle in the parking lot. The police car's flashing lights illuminated the dimly lit area.

"Well, I'm in the colored part of Marmalade, alright." She said before returning to her luggage.

It wasn't until she'd thought she'd heard Zora and Rosa arguing outside, that she hurried and slipped on the first dress her hands landed on. She stuffed her feet into her shoes, then raced outside. She looked over the balcony and gasped at the sight of the women shouting at an officer.

Georgia swiftly ran down the stairs. "What in tarnation is *goin on* down here?"

"Shut up and get back in your room!" The officer immediately shouted at Georgia.

"Just who in the hell do you think you're talkin' to?" She asked, startled at how quickly he had disregarded her. In all of her thirty-three years, she had never been spoken to like that by an officer.

"Georgia," Rosa started. "You don't have to-"

"You listen here, nigra." The officer said sternly, waving a billy club at Georgia. "These two are already in a whole heap of trouble for breakin' curfew-"

"For the last time, we had no idea about a six o'clock curfew in Marmalade!" Zora shouted.

"Curfew?" Georgia asked. "How in the world is curfew being broken if we're not out on the streets?"

"Get your black ass back inside." The officer warned. "I didn't ask for any of your sassin'." He turned his attention to Rosa and Zora. "Now unless you two can show proof that you've paid for rooms at this here inn, I'm gonna have to take you in for breaking curfew."

Zora glared at the officer. "That's just ludicrous! Why in the world would we travel all this way in our swimsuits just to trespass?"

"Put yer hands behind your back. I'm placing all three of you nigras under arrest." He placed a hand on top of his revolver, which was still tucked in his holster.

"Now wait just a goddamn minute." Georgia protested. "Can't you just ask the inn keeper if they paid for rooms?"

"Get yer ass over here!" The officer ordered, yanking Georgia so hard, she thought she heard her neck crack.

"Get your paws offa' me!" Georgia snapped. Rosa and Zora cried out in outrage as the officer handcuffed a bucking Georgia. He then shoved her to the ground.

Zora stared at Rosa. "*Do something.*" She mouthed.

Rosa sighed. She quickly glanced around the pool area and the room windows overlooking the pool. "Alright. That's enough." She said nonchalantly. She then snapped her fingers.

Georgia and the officer were immediately frozen in time. Zora laughed at the sight of the officer, who was now as still as a mannequin, with both his arms lunging towards her.

100

"Now what, tough guy?" Zora taunted, then stuck out her tongue. "You ain't so bad now are you? *What's up?*"

"You know neither one can hear or see you." Rosa reminded.

"I know." Zora shrugged. "Doesn't make it any less fun. What you gonna do this time? Erase their memory? Teleportation?"

Rosa used her thumb and index finger to rub her chin as she thought for second. "Naw. We need Georgia to remember this."

"I got it." Zora said. "Erase this fat lard's memory and teleport his ass on out of here."

"And what about her?" Rosa asked, pointing her chin at Georgia, who was sprawled face down between them.

"Teleport us all back to the room before you unfreeze her. We'll make somethin' up. Tell her she blacked out or somethin' after he pushed her."

"Sound good." Rosa replied. She took in a deep breath, then closed her eyes.

"Wait!" Zora squealed.

Rosa opened her eyes. "What is it?"

Before she knew it, Zora reared her fist back and connected her knuckles to the officer's right eye with such a powerful blow, she almost lost her balance.

"You can teleport his ass up outta here now."

CHAPTER
TWENTY-ONE

Noah threw a twin-sized blanket and a flat pillow at Rusty. "It's all we got. Take it or leave it."

"Thank you, Noah." Rusty replied, grateful to have some cushion to put over his pallet. "Mind unchainin' me? I ain't fixin' to run off nowhere. It's just so uncomfortable when I sleep."

He stared into his blue eyes a minute before releasing a sigh. He pulled out the key to the lock and knelt before him to release him.

"Thank you." Rusty said.

"Please don't make me regret this." Noah said to him.

"Like I told Ida, I gots nowhere to go."

"And you," Noah said sternly, facing Marley, who was sitting right beside Rusty, showing off his G.I. Joe figurine. "What did we say about blabbin' to anyone about Rusty?"

Marley held his head down in shame. "We gotta keep him a secret."

"Right." Noah replied, throwing a pack of Bazookas at Marley's feet. "No more bringin' nobody over here to see nothin', got that?"

Marley nodded excitedly, immediately dropping his figurines to catch the pack of gum.

"Where's Ida and Malcolm? You shouldn't be out here alone." Noah stated.

"I didn't tell 'em I was comin' here."

"Marley, next time—"

Noah was interrupted by a pounding on the door.

"Who is it?!"Noah shouted, walking towards the door.

"It's me!"

"What do ya want, Charlene?" He asked behind the closed door.

"Is Marley in there? Mama's sent me out here to look for him."

"He's in here with me."

"Mama said he needs to come in and take a bath."

Noah looked over at Marley. "You heard her Marley. Go on out and head to the house."

Marley stood up, still holding his gum. He looked down at Rusty. "You can play with my G.I. Joes 'til I come back."

Noah waited for his youngest brother to come to the door before opening the door to the shed.

"What you guys doing in there?" Charlene asked, as she attempted to look around Noah's tall lanky body. "Savannah absolutely refused to come over here to look for Marley."

Ignoring her, Noah gently shoved Marley out and swiftly shut the door in his sister's face.

"Noah McGwire, I'm gonna find out what you all are up to!" Charlene shouted.

CHAPTER
TWENTY–TWO

It was going on two days since Georgia had left. Jimmy had not eaten, gone to work, nor had he had a good night's rest. He had tried driving around town and had even stopped by the Wakefield's to ask Eugenia if she'd seen her best friend.

"No, I haven't seen Georgia." Oliver Wakefield had told him at the door. His face seemed to be drained of color.

"You alright, Oliver?" Jimmy asked, concerned.

Oliver tried his best to plaster on a smile. "I'm dandy."

"Is Eugenia in? I'd love to speak to her for a spell."

Oliver looked over his shoulder, then back at Jimmy. He opened his mouth to speak, then suddenly broke down into tears.

Alarmed, Jimmy shoved past him, expecting to find Eugenia hurt or worse. Instead, he didn't see anyone in their living room.

He walked back over to Oliver, who had shut the door and was now on the ground with his palms covering his face. "What's the matter, Oliver? Where's Eugenia?"

"She's upstairs."

Jimmy rushed up the staircase two steps at a time. He knocked on the only bedroom door he found that was shut. "Eugenia. It's Jimmy. You decent?"

He heard no response.

"Eugenia?!" He shouted, even more alarmed.

"She's decent." He heard Oliver say tearfully, walking behind him.

Jimmy took a moment to brace himself before opening the bedroom door.

"Don't look at me!" Jimmy thought he'd heard Eugenia cry out. Instead he saw a beautiful golden-brown woman with an enormous brown afro curled onto the floor bawling.

Jimmy took a moment to marvel at the size of the large thick afro that sat on her head. Her now course hair was so humungous, he was tempted to pull it, just to see if it were real.

"Eugenia?" Jimmy queried, drawing near. "That you?"

With her dark green eyes filled with tears, she looked up at him. "Yes." She whispered, relieved that he recognized her.

Riddled with guilt that he had almost shot and killed his beloved wife, Oliver cried as he hugged Eugenia.

"Did you call the cops or tell anyone about this?" Jimmy asked.

They both shook their heads.

"Good." Jimmy replied. "I think it'd be best to not tell anyone and to keep her indoors until she changes back. Same thing's happen to Georgia."

Eugenia's eyes filled with hope as looked up at him. "It'll come off? How'd she git' it off?"

Jimmy sighed. "I'm not sure if she's changed back yet. I haven't seen her. She ran off almost two days ago. That's why I came over here."

"How do you know it'll come off?" Oliver inquired.

"Trust me on that." Jimmy assured, not knowing how else to answer.

Eugenia gasped. "I think she came over her earlier today, but I ran her off. I didn't know it was her."

"You sure it was Georgia?" Jimmy asked, before going on to give a description of his wife.

Eugenia nodded, agreeing with his description. "Yep. She had the same blue eyes and her hair was blonde and her skin looked just like a nigger's."

"Same as you do now, right?" Jimmy asked spitefully.

After driving back over to his house, he decided to call the police station to see if she'd been picked up for violating the town's curfew.

"What'd you say your wife's name is, sir?" The clerk asked. He could hear her typing into the computer.

"Georgia. Georgia Daniels."

Her typing stopped. "Is this Jimmy Daniels?" She asked.

"Yes. Yes, it is."

"Oh, Jimmy. There's no way she could've been picked up for curfew. The curfew's only for negroes." She chuckled.

"Would you just do me a solid and double check for me?"

"Alright." He heard more typing, then, "Nope. Just like I thought. She ain't in the system."

"Thank you for checking." He said before hanging up.

"Who was that?"

Jimmy nearly wet himself as he turned towards the voice. "Could you please start using the doorbell like everyone else 'stead of just appearing in my living room?"

"And get caught standing out there after curfew?" Freddie smiled.

"Can't find Georgia. Darn near turned the town upside-down lookin' for her." Jimmy revealed, sitting.

Freddie took a seat beside him. "And she was no where to be found, hunh?"

"Looked everywhere. Molasses is but so big."

"Oh, she's not in Molasses. That's why you're not havin' any luck finding her." Freddie informed.

He looked at Freddie. "What do you mean? Did you see 'er?"

"She's over in the next town."

Jimmy shoulders perked up. "In Marmalade?"

"Yup. I wouldn't worry too much, Jim. She's in good hands." He assured.

Jimmy shot up off the sofa and grabbed Freddie by the front of the shirt as he stood over him. "Where's my wife? Did you do somethin' to her?"

Freddie glanced at Jimmy's grasp on his shirt. "I'd let go now if I were you." He calmly advised.

"Not until you tell me where Georgia is."

Before Jimmy could blink, Freddie had instantly vanished, leaving Jimmy hunched over the sofa holding on to the air.

CHAPTER
TWENTY-THREE

Hours passed before Freddie arrived at the inn to find his sister and girlfriend standing up to braid the coarse hair of a blue-eyed blonde negro woman, who was seated on the motel's chair.

"What took you so long? We were worried about you." Zora said, looking relieved. She gave Freddie a hug. "'I thought something happened."

"It's not safe to be over in Molasses after curfew, little brother." Rosa reminded, greasing Georgia's scalp.

"Sorry 'bout that. Took longer than I expected." He informed. He walked over to Georgia and extended a hand towards her. "How ya' doin', ma'am? I'm Frederick King. Rosa's brother."

Georgia plastered a phony smile across her face. "Georgia Murphy."

"Nice ring you got there. You married?" Freddie asked, admiring the diamond ring.

"Separated." Georgia replied, making a mental note to hide her diamond ring before going to bed. She'd sleep with one eye open if she had to. She would need it to pawn when and if she ran low on cash.

"Got any kids?" Freddie asked.

Georgia was now annoyed. What was with all the questions. She decided then that she would leave first thing in the morning while everyone was still asleep.

"No. Never wanted any." Georgia finally answered.

"Why'd you and your old man separate? If you don't mind me asking?" He probed.

For a split second, she thought she'd seen his eyes flicker blue.

Rosa spoke up. "Girl, you don't have to answer that. Freddie, get out of her business. If she wants us to know, she'll tell us."

"I left him on account of him lying to me about somethin' important." Georgia replied anyway.

Zora raised a brow. "It had to be somethin' real scandalous for you to have left after thirteen years."

Rosa elbowed Zora, just as Georgia looked up at the two women. "How'd you know how long we'd been together?" She asked suspiciously.

"You just told us a minute ago." Rosa quickly lied.

"I did?" She furrowed her brows as she tried to remember doing so.

"Yes. You must be exhausted." Zora added. "Don't worry, we're just about done with your hair."

"You can have my bed tonight." Rosa said to Georgia. "I don't mind sleeping on the floor. Seem like you've had a rough couple of days.

"Thank you. I 'ppreciate that. Where are ya guys from?"

"Some place far far away." Rosa answered.

"Oh? I don't recognize your accents? My husband and I used to travel a lot. We might've visited your hometown before."

"Negus." Freddie answered. Behind Georgia, Rosa and Zora glared at him, to which he simply shrugged.

"Don't think I've ever heard of it. Is it in Mississippi?"

"Nah." Zora replied. "It's over in....Africa."

"Africa?" Georgia repeated, furrowing her brows. She had never met real-life Africans before. Furthermore, these people looked nothing like the starving shoeless African people she often seen on television commercials and magazines with flies buzzing around their faces. "What brings you guys over to these necks of the woods?" She asked suspiciously.

Rosa, Freddie, and Zora all looked at one another. They hadn't prepared to be interrogated.

"We got lost." Rosa replied. "We were on our way to Marietta, when Freddie here, lost our map. Saw how nice Mississippi was and decided to stay for a night."

"I reckon these roads ae a bit tricky, but you might wanna get out of here soon as possible. Not sure if you've heard, but the state of Mississippi is a dangerous place for you coloreds."

"And why is that?" Zora inquired.

"Well," Georgia began. "Folks 'round here just ain't too fond of coloreds."

"But why?" Zora asked.

Georgia thought about how she could tell them in a polite way that negroes were thought of as savages, monkeys, lazy, and of no real use to society.

"We're not savages." Rosa chimed, as if reading Georgia's thoughts. "This country was built on the backs of slaves."

Zora nodded. "I prefer the term *the enslaved*, 'cause that's exactly what they were. Enslaved."

Georgia sat there, feeling uneasy. She didn't know why she felt that way whenever slavery was brought up. "Slavery was such a long time ago. Sometimes I wish we could all just put it past us and move on, ya know what I mean?"

The room fell silent.

Freddie finally spoke up. "You know, I always wondered why whites hated blacks...I mean *negroes*....so much. What did we ever do to them except being born colored? They think we got any control of that?"

"Baby," Zora said to Freddie, "Some of 'em just ain't never learned to think for themselves."

"What do you mean by that?" Georgia asked, feeling herself getting upset.

"What I mean is, some of 'em were taught to hate. You ever seen a white baby and colored baby play together? They can sit there and laugh and play and not even realize that their skin color is any different. It's when they get a little older and their parents get to brainwashin' 'em, that they become so cold-hearted and mean."

Georgia thought about this for a while.

"You're all done, missy. Go on and check it out." Rosa said.

Georgia ran a hand on top of her thick braids before rising. She walked over to the mirror and almost scared herself when she looked at her reflection. She still hadn't gotten used to seeing herself as a mahogany-toned woman.

Georgia hated her hair but couldn't bring herself to tell the ladies. She wanted her bouncy silk ringlets back. They were a lot more manageable and easier on the eyes to her.

"You don't have to like it," Rosa said behind her. "But at least you won't have to worry about them knots and combing your hair for a while."

"And it'll be easier to put a scarf or hat over your head now, if you choose to." Zora added.

Georgia finally smiled. Well at least now she didn't have to walk around with a ridiculous afro. One thing she had learned was that the negro hair took on many forms. She noticed while walking in the rain and again while showering, that her hair would flatten and fall to the center of her back. It had both saddened and amazed her that once dry, her hair sprung back to its original tightly coiled form.

"I'm gonna call it a night." Georgia announced.

"Already?" Zora asked. "'It's barely nine o'clock.

"I'm dog tired." Georgia answered honestly, heading to the bed Rosa had cleared out for her. She was so tired and elated to be laying on a real bed, she completely forgot about how ghastly it was for her to be sleeping on the same linen that a negro had. In fact, within a minute of Georgia's head touching the pillow, she had dozed off into a peaceful rest.

CHAPTER
TWENTY–FOUR

Earline Thompson cracked an eye open to check the time on her alarm clock. She was surprised Dylan hadn't awoken her up for an early morning romp like he usually did.

"Baby?" She groaned, stretching. "Dylan, baby. Get up." She said, finally opening her eyes.

Dylan groaned in response.

"C'mon, baby. Get up. You've got to get ready for work in a few minutes."

With his eyes still closed, he caressed her body over her long silk night gown. "Gimme a coupla' more minutes, Earline."

Earline reached out to shove him, when she caught sight of her arms. "What in God's name!" She gasped.

"What is it?" Dylan asked, finally opening his eyes. He nearly jumped a feet in the air. "Who in tarnation are you?" He asked, reaching for his revolver on the nightstand.

"Dylan, what-"

"Keep yer gotdamn hands up!"

Earline glowered at him. "Quit messin', Dylan. Put that down!"

"Put your fucking hands up!"

"Dylan!" Earline shouted. "You're scaring me! Now quit."

Dylan tackled the cocoa-hued pregnant woman on her stomach. She shouted in agony as he twisted her arm around her back.

"*Get...off ..of me!*" She cried out.

"Not until you tell me what you've done with Earline."

"You're breaking my arm!"

"Who put you up to this?!" He asked. "Was it the nigger down at the sheriff's office?"

"Hunh? What nigger? I haven't a clue what you're talkin' about, Dylan."

"Where's Earline?"

"I *am* Earline!"

He flipped the woman over and placed a hand around her neck. "If you don't tell me where she is right now, I'm gonna skin you alive, then hang you from one of 'em trees out there." He threatened, tightening his grip around her neck.

Earline kicked and screamed, until finally he released his hold on her. He began groaning and she didn't understand why until she saw him hunch over, grabbing his genitals. She realized then that she must've kicked him right in the groin.

Earline hurriedly grabbed his revolver and ran out of her trailer. She headed straight to Penny Thorton's trailer and pounded on the door.

"Penny! Penny!" She cried out, keeping an eye out behind her for any signs of Dylan Ford.

The door to the trailer flew open.

"Hey Earline. What are you doing over her so earl-AHHH!" Penny shouted. She tried shutting the door, but Earline, wielding a revolver, caught the door open with her arm.

Earline bombarded her way in and promptly locked the door behind her. Her legs felt as if it were made of gelatin, as she checked through the window to see if Dylan had followed her. He was nowhere in sight.

"Please don't kill me!" Penny shouted hysterically, falling to the ground. "I've never wronged you people! I grew up on the south side!"

Earline looked taken aback. "You grew up on the south side? With the niggers?"

Penny nodded, wishing Raymond hadn't left for work so early. "Yes. My very first boyfriend were a colored boy and my best friend was also colored. I'm not like these other white people. Please don't kill me."

"Get up and quit that whimperin'! You sound like a wounded dog. I'm not here to shoot you. I just need to hide from Dylan."

Penny eyes widened. "Dylan Ford?"

"Well, who else?" Earline snapped.

"Did somethin' happen over there?" She asked, wishing she hadn't left her brand new shot gun in the bedroom.

"Yes! That sonofabitch tried to kill me. Bad enough I woke up to my arms lookin like this. I gotta head down to Dr. Boone's office later to get this checked out."

Penny gasped, already suspecting the worse. "Did you kill her?" She thought of Shirley, then Earline. It made sense that the killer would come for her next.

"Kill who? Why is everyone actin' so strange?" She asked, pacing the room. It wasn't until she caught her reflection in the small mirror hanging in the living room, did she halt in her steps.

"Oh....my....god." She patted her short dark brown afro as her mouth hung open.

Convinced that the woman was mental, Penny began reciting The Lord's Prayer. "*Art Father, which art in heaven...*"

"Oh my gawd! Oh my....Jesus Christ!" Earline cried, waving the revolver recklessly in the air.

"Thy kingdom come..."

"Where's 'yer rubbin' alcohol? I need to scrub this—oh, just look at my hair!"

"On earth, as it is in heaven..."

The sudden pounding at the door hushed Earline.

"Give us this day, our daily bread..."

"Penny." Earline whispered kneeling beside her.

"And forgive us our debts, as we forgive our debtors..."

"Penny!" Earline called out through gritted teeth.

With tears in her eyes, Penny made eye contact with the woman. "Go ahead. Kill me. Just make it quick, please." She sniffled.

"Someone's at the door. Look and see who it is." Earline instructed.

Both women stood to their feet and headed towards the door. "Just look out the peephole and tell see who it is." She repeated.

Penny did as she was told. She looked at Earline. "It's Dylan Ford."

"Aw shoot!"

"Penny, are you in there?" They heard the detective ask. *"I'm fixin' to call for back up and bust this door down if you don't open up! Just wanna make sure you're alright!"*

Penny looked at the woman helplessly.

"Tell 'em you're home." Earline instructed.

Penny nodded as she reached for the door.

Earline swatted her hands away from the door knob. "No. I didn't say to open the door. Just tell 'em."

"Penny? You there? It's Dylan."

"I'm here, detective." Penny shouted.

"Could you open the door?"

Again, she looked at her kidnapper, waiting for further instructions.

Earline sighed. "Alright, I want you to open the door just wide enough for him to see your face, but do not let him in." She pointed her revolver at Penny. "You let him in and I won't hesitate to pull this trigger. Got that?"

Penny nodded.

"Wipe your eyes 'fore you open that door. Don't want him being suspicious any."

"Penny? You there?"

With Earline Thompson hiding to the left of her, Penny cracked open the door. "What is it? I'm kinda busy right now, detective."

"Have you seen Earline?"

"Git rid of 'em." Earline whispered.

"Earline? No, can't say I have." She blinked rapidly at him. Hoping he'd figure out that something was wrong.

Detective Ford furrowed his brows. "Sure everything's okay in there?"

"Everything's just fine. I'm just a little tired is all."

He stared at her for a moment longer. "You mind if I take a look inside yer trailer?"

"Now's really not a good time, detective." She answered, blinking rapidly. She didn't want to be left alone with a kidnapper and possible murderer.

He sighed. "Look, Penny, I found a strange nigger in our trailer this morning and now Earline's nowhere to be found."

"You don't say? What do you suppose happened?" She asked, feeling a mixture of concern and fear.

"Git rid of 'em I said." She heard Earline whisper.

"I'm sure that nigger did somethin' to her. I'm gonna go ahead and call the police station to get a search party started."

A *search party*? Earline thought. Last thing she needed was a whole bunch of cops snooping around here. *"Tell 'em you've heard from me."* She whispered.

"What?" Penny asked, looking directly at her.

Earline placed her finger on the trigger.

"I said I'm gonna go ahead and call the police station to get a search party started." Ford repeated.

"I just remembered. Earline *did* stop by bright and early this morning."

"She did?" He asked.

"Yes. The sun wasn't even up yet when she stopped by."

"Before the sun come up, you say?" He asked, curiously. "Doesn't sound like the woman I know. Did she say where she was headed?"

"To your place!" Penny quickly answered.

Earline groaned. Now, why'd she go and say that for? She abruptly shut the front door between them.

Detective Ford immediately began pounding on the door.

Earline pressed the revolver to the side of Penny's head. "Tell 'em you'll call him if you hear anything else." She whispered.

Penny immediately did as instructed.

"Penny! Where'd you say she say was headed?" He asked again, from the other side of the door.

"Just ignore 'em. He'll go away. I need to figure out what I'm gone' do."

118

CHAPTER

TWENTY-FIVE

"Aw, fudge." Georgia muttered. She was disappointed to find that she had overslept. Her plan was to wake up before dawn and hitch hike as far away from Saint Molasses as possible. Instead, she had awoken to Rosa, Zee, and Freddie staring intently at the inn's black and white television.

"Anybody got the time?" She asked.

Rosa detached herself from the T.V. long enough to look at her watch. "It's almost noon. Did we wake you? I told them to keep it down."

"No, not at all."

She walked over to Georgia. "Good. I left you some fruit salad over there by the coffeemaker. I didn't wanna wake you. You looked so peaceful."

"Don't you people eat anything other than nuts and fruits?"

Rosa laughed. "We're raw vegans."

"You're what?"

"Raw vegans. Means we don't eat any dairy, meat, processed food or anything that comes from animals."

Great, Georgia thought, sitting up. "Thought you guys were leaving bright and early?"

Still facing the television, Freddie spoke up. "She wouldn't let us wake you up."

Georgia looked incredulously at Rosa. "You didn't have to stay on account of me."

Rosa furrowed her brows. "And just leave you here? Couldn't do that."

"Well, thanks, but I reckon I would've been just fine. I'm not a stranger to Marmalade and Saint Molasses."

Rosa smiled. "Girl, that don't make no difference to us. Freddie, Zee, and I are good people. We raised to look after each other and anyone in need. Besides, you said so yourself that Mississippi wasn't a place for a negro to get into trouble. Now suppose the innkeeper had found you in here after we checked out?"

"Guess you got a point there." She admitted.

Rosa looked over at the television. "She still in there?" She asked Freddie and Zora.

"Yep." Freddie answered.

Yawning, Georgia asked, "What are you guys watchin'?"

"Hostage situation at Meadowbrook." Zora replied.

"Meadowbrook Square? The trailer park?" Georgia asked, kicking the covers off of her.

"Looks like it." Freddie answered, just as Georgia and Rosa joined them.

"Oh, my word." Georgia said, covering her mouth with her hands. "That's Penny Thornton's trailer. Do they know who's got her hostage?"

"Out-of-towner." Freddie answered.

"Oh, look!" Zora exclaimed, although their eyes were all glued to the screen. "They're releasing the hostage!"

CHAPTER
TWENTY – SIX

Detective Edward Bailey cursed under his breath as soon as he'd seen the barricade around Penny Thorton's trailer. He had practically flown across town so he could arrive to the trailer park before anyone else, as soon as he'd hung up with Ford earlier.

After calling in the sheriff's office for backup, Detective Ford had called Bailey and told him about the negro he'd found in Earline's bed.

"How'd she look?" Bailey had asked over the phone, tentatively.

"I don't know. Everything just happened so fast."

"Was she wearin' Earline's clothes?"

"Yes. That wench had on the audacity to put on the same night gown Earline had put on to bed."

"Have you called it in yet?" Bailey asked.

"Called the sheriff's office soon as that nigger ran off with muh' gun." Ford answered. He tried his best to collect himself before continuing, "And I can't find Earline. I think she's been kidnapped, Bailey."

"I'm getting dressed as we speak. I'll be right over."

That had only been less than ten minutes ago. The whole time he had driven to Meadowbrook Square, he couldn't stop thinking about what Barney Harper had told him at the sheriff's office.

"Penny Thornton was just released." Ford informed, as soon as Bailey had arrived to the scene. "I knew somethin' was off when she slammed the door in my face. It's not like Penny at all to do somethin' as unruly as that."

"Where is she?" Bailey asked.

Ford pointed over to the medics, where Penny was sitting up on the back of an ambulance. "Still can't find Earline. Penny said she made the whole bit up about seeing her this morning."

"*Dylan Bartholomew Ford!*" They both heard a woman's voice call out behind them.

"Shit!" Ford cursed, immediately recognizing the voice before turning.

Bailey took a few steps back as he watched Moriah Ford, donned in a yellow and pink floral minidress and white patent leather go-go boots quickly make her way towards her husband. She marched right up to Dylan and slapped his face so hard, she left a bright pink hand print on his left cheek.

"She's pregnant?!" Moriah shouted.

Bailey's eyes bulged at the revelation. Until now, he hadn't known that Dylan had gotten Earline pregnant.

"What?" Ford asked, feigning ignorance. "Moriah, what are you-"

"Don't you even fix your pie-hole to lie to me, Dylan! It's all over the news!"

"Moriah-"

She swiftly slapped his face again. "Do you know how embarrassin' it is hear on the news that the missin' woman is expectin' and that *my* husband's the one that done knocked her up?"

"Moriah, can we talk about this-"

"I was at Roseanne's getting my hair shampooed when the news announced it." She added through gritted teeth.

Bailey left the quarreling couple to themselves and was about to make his way over to Penny, when he overheard Deputy Aiken instruct his men to get ready to shoot.

"Suspect fixin' to come out?" He asked Deputy Aiken.

The deputy shook his head. "Damn jigaboo refuses to come out. Have no choice but to shoot right through that trailer."

"What about tear gas? Wouldn't it be better to catch her alive?" He asked, concerned. "So we can get some important info on Earline's whereabouts?"

"We've already tried getting her to cooperate." The deputy replied.

"But deputy, she's with child."

Deputy Aiken's brows furrowed. "Ford nor the hostage said anything about 'er being pregnant, not that it matters any. Be one less darkie in the world."

"*You got one more chance to come out with your hands up!*" He heard an officer shout through a megaphone. The officer then looked back at the deputy. The deputy nodded and gave the officer a thumbs up.

"Wait!" Bailey shouted. He looked frantically at the deputy, then ran towards the officer. "Hold on a minute!" He shouted, but his words were drowned by the sound of at least two dozen shots being fired.

"Nooo!" Bailey cried out in anguish, dropping to his knees.

CHAPTER
TWENTY–SEVEN

"*T*he female suspect has been shot! I repeat, the female suspect that held local Molasses resident, Penny Thorton, hostage for
three terrifying hours, has been shot down by local authorities. Earline Thompson, another local resident, is being reported as still
missing. This makes it the fourth missing persons' case for the
trailer community and the sixty-sixth missing person for Toby
county. So far, there has been a total of seventy arrests related to
intruders. Nineteen out of the seventy were shot down by police.
Due to overpopulation, over half of the intruders have been trans-
ported over to the city of Marmalade's county jail."*

Jimmy stood cemented in front of the television stunned.
He could not believe he'd just witnessed Earline Thompson,
a long-time Saint Molasses resident, get massacred on live
television. Riddled with sudden guilt, he fell to his knees and
cried into his palms. He hadn't really known Earline. Heck
he'd never even spoken a word to her, but he couldn't help
feeling partly responsible nonetheless.

*I should've said something long ago. I should've called the detec-
tives and told them everything.* He thought to himself. He worried about Georgia and whether she was safe or still alive
wherever she'd run off to.

Unable to suppress his rage any longer, he jumped up and
knocked a vase off of an end table. Then another vase. He

stomped over to the posh paintings on the wall. "That fucking Freddie!" He shouted tearfully, smashing paintings onto
the ground.

*If it weren't for Freddie, this town wouldn't be upside down
right now.* He thought.

Not only was their usually quiet town in disarray, but his
beloved wife had run out on him. He'd heard that his boss
and other colleagues had stop showing up for work. Some had
gone missing. The town was on a brink of collapse, and it
was all Freddie's fault.

Taking in deep rapid breaths, he took a moment to com-
pose himself. He thought long and hard before deciding to
phone the one person he knew he could always count on to
lend him an ear.

"Lord, pigs must be flying outside! Is it really you?"

Jimmy sighed. "Yes, ma, it's me."

"Ben! Guess who's on the phone?" He heard his mother ask.
"It's Jamey. Yes, your son, James."

"I can give you ring later, Ma, if you're-"

"Horsefeathers! Everything alright, Jamey? Ya not sick
or anything, are ya'?"

"Everything's fine, ma."

 "I'm so happy to hear from you. When are you comin' to
Dayton to visit? We haven't seen you since your brother's
funeral, may he rest in peace, and that was almost fifteen
years ago, son."

"Might be comin' up that way sooner than you think.
How's Benny Jr. and Abigail?"

"They're doing just dandy. You have a brand-new
nephew. Abigail and her husband just had their sixth boy. He
was just born coupla' days ago on the thirteenth. You should
give your brother and sister a call sometime, son. You need
their number?"

"No, ma'am. I have their number, ma."

"He done picked up a southern accent, too." He heard her say to his father. "Hol' on a minute Jamey, your father wants to speak with you."

"James?" Jimmy nearly cried at the sound of his father's voice. He wondered if his father still looked like an exact replica of Elvis Presley. He hadn't known just how much he missed his family until now. The last time he'd call his parents was about two years ago, in '67, when interracial marriage had become legalized nationwide.

"Yeah, pops. It's me."

"Been too long, son. Gotta call more often. Even if it's just to speak to your mother." His father instructed.

Jimmy nodded, forgetting his father could not see him. "Okay, pops."

"Answer somethin' for me son. Your brother, Benny, seems to have the notion that you're married with children? You know your mother would have a fit if you ran off and got married without her meeting the new bride."

"Yes, pops. Got married about nine years ago. We don't have any youngins yet. Georgia, that's my wife, she isn't ready to have any just yet."

"He said yes." He heard his father confirm to his mother. "Hold on, son. Your mother wants to say something."

Jimmy sucked in a breath. He closed his eyes as he braced himself for the worse.

"Jamey, say it ain't so? You done found a wife and had you some young?"

Jimmy promptly exhaled, relieved that he could hear his mother's smile over the phone.

"No kids yet, ma. Just a wife."

"Well what's her name? What she look like?"

"Her name is Georgia and she's gorgeous."

126

"Your father and I would love for you and your wife to come visit us sometime before the good Lord calls us home."

"Aw, don't talk like that, ma."

"Tell me more about this Georgia. Where is she from? What kind of people she come from?"

"Uh, she's from South Carolina. Her family is pretty well known down in the Carolinas. They run the largest furniture business in the south."

"Furniture business you say?"

"Yes, ma'am?"

"In South Carolina?"

"Yes, ma'am."

"Sounds kinda strange for them southern whites to allow coloreds to make more money than them. Don't you remember how many times your father's store was burned to a crisp by the klan? And your father's a white man. Thought things were worse in the south."

"Oh, they are. Still is. Georgia isn't colored, ma'. She's white."

Mrs. Daniels chuckled. "Well I reckon I got me a black and a white daughter-in-law now. When are you comin' to Dayton so we can meet 'er?"

Jimmy's throat tightened. He couldn't bring himself to tell her that his wife had left as soon as she'd found out he had been passing for white the whole time they'd been together.

"Hello? You still there, Jamey?"

"I'm here, ma. I'll let you know when I can get some time off of work."

"I'm so happy you finally found someone who accept you for who you are. You know, your father and I were always worried about you, on account of you being our only child with white skin. You know not all negro women like a man who looks white and not all white women like a black man, period." She chuckled. "I'm just happy you found you a woman who accept you for who you are."

"Me too, ma."

"Is there a number we can call to speak to you? The last number you gave us was no good. I think your brother might've written it down wrong."

Jimmy recited the number to his home phone. Now that Georgia was gone, he was no longer hesitant about giving his family the correct number.

With Mrs. Daniel still rambling on the other end of the line, Jimmy's brows furrowed as his eyes caught sight of the five o'clock news.

"Ma, I really have to go. Tell pops I said I'll give him a ring later." He didn't even wait for his mother to hang up before he turned up the volume of the television.

"*What you are seeing here, ladies and gents, is another police barricade on the south side. We've just received word from Deputy Aikens that the Hayne's killer has been caught! I repeat, the murderer of Russell and Judith Haynes, has just been caught!*"

CHAPTER

TWENTY-EIGHT

Noah stepped off the bus with a little pep in his step. He sang the lyrics to a Marvin Gaye song as he headed home. Not only had he gotten a five-cent raise, but Imani Cooper had finally agreed to see *Midnight Cowboy* with him next weekend. He was on such a high, feeling as if he were walking on cloud-nine, that he almost didn't notice the large crowd surrounding his parent's home.

He spotted his parents, Marley, and his two older sisters behind the yellow police tape in front of their front yard.

"What's goin' on?" He asked his family.

His mother stared at him. "Did you know about the fugitive hiding in the shed?"

Noah's heart dropped. He looked at Marley, who had tears rolling down his cheeks.

"Marley had nothin' to do with this. I called the sheriff's office." Charlene said angrily. "I knew you all were up to no good. We all could've been murdered, Noah!"

"He's not dangerous."

His father glowered at him from his wheelchair. "He's a *murderer*, son. What the hell were you thinking?"

"I-I'm sorry. I thought we could use the reward money."

Mrs. McGwire wiped the tears from her eyes. "You should've told us. We could've called the police as soon as you found him."

129

"Ma, I'm sorry." Noah glanced around the yard filled with cops and neighbors. "Where's Malcolm and Ida?"

"They're still in there!" Charlene said, bursting into tears.

"They're in there with the killer." Mr. McGwire commented. "You must feel real proud of yourself right now."

With anger rising in him, Noah stormed off towards the shed. He tried bending below the yellow police tape but was stopped by a plain-clothed officer.

"Hey! You can't go in there!" He shouted.

Noah halted. "My brother and sister is in there."

The man raised a brow. "Are you Noah McGwire?'

"Yes, sir." He answered uneasily.

"I'm Detective Bailey." He said, retrieving a pen and pad from his pocket. "What's your relation to the suspect?"

"There is no relation."

"Were you there the morning of the murders?"

Noah crinkled his forehead. "What? No, man."

"Mr. McGwire, I'm sorry but we're gonna have to take you in for questioning."

"What?" Noah asked. He looked over in the distance at his family, just as a news van was pulling up. "Mama!" He shouted, getting his family's attention. "They're trying to take me in!"

Savannah, running across the front yard in her house slippers, caught up to them first. "Why are you arresting my brother? He ain't had nothin' to do with this."

Detective Bailey summoned Detective Ford for assistance. "We're not arresting Mr. McGwire. We're taking him in for questioning."

"Stand back!" Detective Ford instructed the family, who had just joined them.

"We need everyone to move back please." A uniformed police woman requested. "The suspect and the hostages are coming out. We wanna make sure no one gets hurt."

"Is he armed?" Detective Ford asked the officer.

Noah answered before she could. "No! There's no weapons in there!"

The officer glared at Noah, then answered the detective. "We're not sure." She looked at Noah again as she continued, "All we know is that he is considered highly dangerous. Now move back!" She ordered.

Noah and his family were pushed away from the front yard and onto the street, where reporters were interviewing the sheriff and neighbors.

"We don't know how many deaths this outsider is responsible for." He heard the sheriff say. "We're working on getting all of that information. We're doing our best to find all missing residents of this town."

"He's just released the two hostages!" A reporter shouted from behind them.

Noah turned and ran back towards his home. He heard his mother's wails as Ida and Malcolm slowly walked out, hand in hand. They looked over at him before they were swarmed by the family, cops, and news crew.

A horrible thought suddenly crossed Noah's mind. What if the boy had completely transformed back into his original color and hair? They would surely charge them for the kidnapping of Rusty Haynes Jr. and possibly for the deaths of the Haynes.

"Suspect's coming out!" He heard Deputy Aiken shout.

"Let's get 'em." He thought he'd heard an officer say.

The police woman from earlier glared at Noah. "Hey, didn't' I tell you to get ba-"

The rapid fire of gunshots startled both Noah and the officer. She shouted for him to get on the ground as she grabbed her gun. Shrieks and shouts from the residents and news crew filled the air as neighbors ran for cover.

Noah squeezed his eyes shut and stayed on the ground until he heard the cries of his youngest brother.

"*Rustyyyy!* They shot Rusty!"

CHAPTER

TWENTY–NINE

"**I** gotta do something." Jimmy said to himself. He turned off the television and grabbed the keys to his Thunderbird. He wasn't sure exactly where the McGwires lived, but he knew it was somewhere in the south side and Saint Molasses was but so big. All he knew for sure was that he could not live with another life taken on his conscience. He would do the right thing and tell the officials, as well as everyone else, about everything.

Rushing to his automobile, Jimmy hadn't even notice Freddie leaning against the passenger door of the Thunderbird, until he spoke. "Sup, Jimmy?"

Jimmy did a double-take. "You! What are *you* doing here? I oughta call the cops! Where's my wife?"

"I'm doing good. How about yourself?" Freddie replied.

Jimmy stormed to where Freddie stood. He poked his head out at Freddie, with his face just inches away. "You reckon I'm shuckin' and jivin' with ya, boy?"

"Get in the car, Jimmy. We're wasting time."

"*We?*" Jimmy asked.

"You're going to the McGwires, right?"

Jimmy stood glaring at the young man a second longer before walking around to the driver's side of the Thunderbird. Knowing that the only way he could get to Georgia was through Freddie, he reluctantly unlocked the passenger side door to let him in.

Jimmy immediately turned on the radio to see if any of the stations would mention the address of the McGwires. *"We've just gotten word that Julia Haynes-Montgomery, the only living child of Russell and Judith Haynes, has just landed at Biloxi International Airport. Now you may have seen Julia on a national television program two days ago claiming that she was raising money for her plane ticket to Mississippi. Well it looks like she finally raised that money. Mrs. Haynes has also scrutinized the Saint Molasses Sheriff's Office for their lack of effort in finding her brother, Russell Haynes, Jr. Sheriff Colin Woods later responded to those allegations, admitting that the Sheriff's Department is simply understaffed."*

"You missed the turn." Freddie informed.

Jimmy looked over at him. "You know your way there? Wait, of course you do." He muttered sarcastically.

"Been there a time or two to keep an eye on young Rusty. Waited 'til everyone was asleep."

Jimmy's jaws tightened. "You know this whole fiasco, this whole mess, could've been avoided if you would've just spoken to the authorities."

"And tell them what? Make another left at this stop sign."

Jimmy made the left. "You could've told them everything you told me."

"You're kidding, right? They'd try to put me in a looney bin. That or area 51. Not that they could anyway. Thank goodness for teleportation."

"Do you realize how many innocent people have died?"

"Innocent? I beg to differ. Besides, I told you already, there's no such thing as death. Anyway, it almost always takes some sort of sacrifice for the greater good to happen." Freddie reminded. "Drive straight ahead. We're almost there."

"What in tarnation?" Jimmy whispered, as his Thunderbird crept near the enormous crowd. A news van as well as several police vehicles and an ambulance were parked on the street.

Jimmy exited the car and was surprised to see officers arresting several outraged residents, both coloreds and whites.

"He was unarmed!" A white resident shouted in despair.

"They shot 'em!" Someone else cried out.

Jimmy looked at Freddie, who was also walking towards the crowd beside him.

"Surprised to see a few white faces, hunh?"

"Very." Jimmy admitted.

Freddie placed a hand on Jimmy's shoulder. "You see, some of these white folks know what's going on. They've either woken up colored and had a change of heart, or they have family members who've changed or been shot down by the law. Not sure if you've noticed, but some of these colored folks here, weren't always colored."

Jimmy halted in his step. "Hey, isn't that...?" He looked towards the street, where a twenty-something-year-old brunette white woman had just stepped out of a cab.

"Yep." Freddie confirmed. "That's her alright."

135

CHAPTER
THIRTY

Noah looked beyond the police tape. For a moment, everything around him froze as he spotted a brown lifeless body sprawled on the ground in front of the shed.

"*Why did they shoot?*" He heard his neighbor from next door, Virginia Berry, sob.

He watched as the angry mob grew and as several members of Malik's militant group were being detained face down on the pavement. Ida, who was being restrained by several officers, shouted tearfully, "We told y'all he wasn't armed! Why'd you have to shoot 'em!"

"Get your hands off my sister!" Noah shouted. The tall lanky McGwire boy ran towards the officer, but was tackled to the ground by another officer.

"Please let my babies go!" Mrs. McGwire pleaded, causing even more outrage throughout the mob.

"Get these people away from here." Deputy Aiken ordered an officer. "We don't need another Watts riot on our hands."

Marley bucked on the grass as he cried uncontrollably. Savannah tried holding him, but he kicked and screamed, then ran past the yellow tape to Rusty's body.

"Hey!" Deputy Aiken hollered. "Someone get him!"

"Don't touch 'em!" Malcolm shouted at the officers. "I'll get 'em." He sprinted towards Marley and Rusty, as Savannah halted in her steps.

Deputy Aiken called over a paramedic. "Soon as he gets the boy, take the body on out of here, will ya?"

Malcolm's eyes teared as he watched his youngest brother cry on Rusty's chest.

"Don't die, Rusty. Please don't die." Marley whispered.

"Marley." Rusty groaned.

"*Oh my God.*" Both Malcolm and Marley were surprised to hear a soft voice behind them.

Rusty's eyes slowly fluttered open. He willed himself to stay conscious as he tried to correct his blurred vision. The figure, now standing over him, resembled an angel. "*Julia?*"

"Your face." She said, inspecting his dark pigment. She looked over at his neck, arms, and legs which were the only parts of him in their original pale color. "What-what happened?" She asked tearfully.

"I-I..." He whispered.

"He's alive!!" Julia shouted at the deputy.

"Hurry! We need to get 'em to a hospital!" Malcolm hollered.

CHAPTER

THIRTY-ONE

"**M**s. Haynes-"

"It's *Mrs. Montgomery!*" Julia shouted tearfully at Deputy Aiken. They both watched the medical personnel carefully place Rusty's barely conscious body onto the stretcher.

"Julia." Deputy Aiken began. "I can assure you that we'll do our best to find your brother's body."

Julia's long brunette hair dangled from left to right as she slowly shook her head at the deputy. She squinted up at him, as she whispered, "But I've-we've already found him."

"I can't imagine how difficult this must be for you." It was obvious that he hadn't heard a word she'd said.

The rest of the deputy's words faded to the background as tears sprung to her eyes. Her head throbbed at the possibility of her losing touch with reality. Had she yearned to be reunited with her only kin so bad, she'd imagined it?

"Julia? Yer there?"

She looked up, expecting to see the deputy, but instead stood face to face with Detective Bailey. She looked around the area for the deputy. Just to be sure she wasn't, indeed, losing her mind.

"The deputy asked me to keep an eye on you. He's over there speaking to the McGwires." He pointed a few feet away to where the deputy was speaking to a colored man in an old wheelchair, and a woman in a white uniform.

"You alright?" Bailey asked, concerned.

"I think so." She replied, but he noticed the same dazed look in her eyes taking over.

Detective Bailey inhaled deeply, then released a nervous breath. "Julia, we need to talk about Rusty." He began. "There's something I think you ought to know."

From across the crowded lawn, Jimmy and Freddie watched as Detective Baily and Julia Haynes walked towards a blue Dodge Monaco. Meanwhile Deputy Aikens had just threatened to release tear gas into the crowd if everyone refused to disperse.

"Should we leave?" Jimmy asked. He couldn't help feeling a bit helpless. He didn't know what he'd thought he could accomplish by driving there.

"Not yet." Freddie said.

"Think the boy will make it?" He asked Freddie. He knew the sight of thirteen-year-old Rusty's discolored bloody body would forever be ingrained in his memory.

Glimpsing into the future, Freddie's eyes flashed from dark brown to blue, then back to brown again. "Time will surely tell." He answered. He squinted into the distance. "There she is." He said, pointing towards a small group forming on the side of the road.

Georgia, Rosa, Zora, and two male teenagers stood at the center of the crowd.

"What in tarnation is she doing?" Jimmy wondered. He walked towards them until he was within earshot of the teens speaking to the crowd.

"Those pigs just shot him down for no reason! What we've all just witnessed was a firing squad." One of the teens said. He had a large afro and wore a black shirt with the words BLACK POWER printed in bold white letters. "We all know Mr. Haynes was a member of the klan. It could have very well been self-defense!"

A few mumbles of agreement could be heard through the crowd.

It was then that Jimmy noticed a male journalist and a female news reporter standing directly across from the angry teens.

"Would you state your name for us?" The woman asked.

"Brother Asaad Shakur. This here-" He pointed at the lanky teen beside him, "Is Brother Malik Abdullah. What we'd like to know is what happened to innocent until proven guilty in this country? This is why we need something like the Black Panther Party here in Molasses. To take care of our own. Who's protecting our community from the police?"

The white female reporter turned to Georgia. "And what about you, ma'am. Did you see anything before the shooting occurred? Any aggressive behavior by the suspect, anything like that?"

Rosa wrapped an arm around Georgia as she answered. "They just shot him down like ...like...like an animal! He's not who they think he is. He's a victim! You can't just go around shooting people down before getting all the facts!"

"You say *he's* the victim?" The reporter asked.

"Mind if I say something?" Jimmy heard himself interrupt.

"Jimmy Daniels." The reporter eyes lit up with surprise. She, as well as the news crew, swiftly turned their attention towards the affluent white resident. "Mr. Daniels, what do you want to say?"

He inhaled deeply, then exhaled as he looked nervously into the camera. "Something very strange has happened in Saint Molasses and a lot of you whites know this. Some of us are hiding out at home, many have fled, and others are trying to find answers."

"Answers to what exactly?" The reporter queried.

"There is a phenomenon goin' on in our town where white residents are...... *changing*."

"Come again?"

"If it hasn't happened to you or anyone you know, God bless you. For those of you it has happened to, this message is for you. Until you've fixed the inside, the disdain you have for coloreds, you'll be stuck as a colored. Simple as that."

"This peckerwood's done lost it." He heard Asaad say.

"It's true." Georgia chimed. She stood beside Jimmy. "It's happened to me. Everyone knows Jimmy and you all know me. I'm Georgia Daniels." She smiled at Jimmy. "Jimmy's wife. That half-colored boy we all seen on that stretcher is Rusty Haynes. This skin-changing phenomenon happened to me. The only way to get back to normal is to start from the inside out."

The reporter, who was afraid to admit that it had happened to her husband and mother-in-law, looked at Georgia as she asked, "And how do you know that'll work for sure?"

"Cause it's happening to me." Georgia admitted softly. She slowly pulled down the collar of her dress to expose the pale pigmentation of her upper chest. She then pulled up her sleeves as far as she could to show her shoulders. They were a light honey color and a noticeable contrast to the rest of the darker mahogany hues on her body. Her shoulders were gradually transforming back to its original color.

"Them same changes done also happened to my boy, Ace, too." A woman shouted from the crowd. "My husband kicked him out, though he knew it was our son. Said he couldn't share the same roof with a darkie. Next morning, my husband woke up colored and now Ace is back in our house."

"It's happening to me." A colored man spoke out. "I wasn't colored a week ago and I'm slowly changing back. What the Daniels are saying is the truth."

"My husband and children have turned to negros as well!" A woman who lived in Meadowbrook Square revealed. "I had to stop my husband from killin' hisself the first time he looked in the mirror. I had to keep the kids outta school on account of this mess. When will this be over?" She asked the Daniels.

"It's up to the person who's changed to determine that." Jimmy answered, looking at his wife.

CHAPTER
THIRTY-TWO

"*Jimmy!*" Georgia called out excitedly. "They're pulling up the driveway!"

"How do I look?" Jimmy asked, racing down the stairs two steps at a time. He halted beside his wife, who stood in front of the door.

She ran her hands down the front of his lapel. "You look perfect."

"Now remember what I told you about my folks. Pops is cool, but ma is-"

"A little over protective." Georgia interrupted. "I know. I got it."

The electric buzzing of the doorbell sounded, confirming the arrival of the older Daniels. Jimmy glanced nervously towards Georgia, inhaled deeply, then pulled the door open.

"Lordy, lordy, lordy!" Marcia Daniels exclaimed. Her short meaty arms reached out to hug him. "My Jamey!"

Georgia smirked in amusement as she watched her husband crouch low enough to accept the four-foot nine woman's embrace.

"You didn't have to get all gussied up for us." Benjamin Daniels informed his son.

Jimmy separated from his mother's embrace to hug his pops, who seemed to have aged tremendously. The last time he had seen them both was in '54 to bury his youngest

143

brother, Louis. They had both had only specks of grey at the time. He could see now that their greys had taken over throughout the years.

Behind him, Georgia cleared her throat.

"Forgive me. Ma, pops, I'd like you to meet my wife, Georgia." Jimmy said. He stepped to the side and allowed Georgia to step forward.

Mr. and Mrs. Daniels both gasped.

"How ya doin'?" Georgia greeted.

Unable to speak, Mr. & Mrs. Daniels simply stared at Georgia's pale olive legs, arms, hands, and neck. Mr. Daniels' head slightly protruded as he squinted at Georgia's golden-brown face. His own warm beige face broke into a smile, as he eyed Georgia's full blonde afro.

"Nice to meet you, Mr. and Mrs. Daniels." Georgia greeted again sheepishly. She stuck out her hand to the older Daniels, but was met with an open-mouth stare from Mrs. Daniels and an amused smirk from Mr. Daniels.

"Ma, Pops?" Jimmy intervened.

Mr. Daniels suddenly broke out into a full out guffaw as he pointed at Georgia. "I reckon-I reckon- I ain't-I ain't never seen-" He tried to speak, but the more he attempted to, the redder his pale face grew and the funnier she looked to him. He finally gave up and bent over as he hooted with laughter, his whole face as red as a strawberry.

Georgia's eyes welled with tears as she glanced at Jimmy.

"Come on, Pops." Jimmy pleaded. "Knock it off."

Still bent over, Mr. Daniels raised a hand in an apology as he tried to collect himself. "I'm sorry, darlin'."

"Come in." Jimmy insisted.

Still embarrassed by the awkward first impression, Georgia held on to Jimmy's arm as the older couple shuffled inside. "You promised me you would tell them before they got here." She chastised in a whisper.

"I *did*." He whispered back.

"Jamey, this house is magnificent!" Mrs. Daniels gushed. She stared at the lavish décor in awe.

"*Jamey?*" Georgia snickered.

Mr. Daniels nodded in agreement. "You've done very well 'fer yourself, son. I'm proud of ya'."

"So am I." Mrs. Daniels added. She walked over by the front door, to where the couple still stood. She grabbed Georgia's hand as she stated, "I'm sorry for earlier. Jamey told us about your-uh-transformation and whatnot, but it's just, we ain't never seen a negro head on a white woman's body befo'."

Georgia plastered on her best smile. "I understand, Mrs. Daniels."

"Call me, mama. You's family. Come 'ere and give me a hug, gal." Mrs. Daniels pulled her in an embrace.

"I appreciate that, ma'am." Georgia replied, as soon as they had separated from their hug.

"I especially wanna apologize 'fer Ben." Mrs. Daniel offered, glancing at her husband behind her, who was now admiring the artwork on the wall.

"Oh, it's alright." Georgia said.

"It's just that, when this small town made national-*hell*-global news, it downright seemed like somethin' straight out of a comic book." She suddenly peered at the younger woman for so long, Georgia swiped a hand over her nose, suddenly insecure.

"What is it Ma?"

"How long ya' say you been this way?"

145

Georgia looked at Jimmy before shaking her head. "I dunno. 'Bout five weeks or so?"

"Sound about right." Jimmy confirmed.

"I thought the news reported that the effects wear off afta' while?"

"Yes, ma. It does." Jimmy answered, moving her along to the living room. "The inner change brings about the outer change."

Marcia Daniels pointed a thumb at Georgia, who was fidgeting nervously beside Jimmy. "Well how come she's still colored? Is you still a racist, gal?"

Taken aback, Georgia immediately shook her head. "No, ma'am. Absolutely not."

"Well then how do ya explain-"

"Ma." Jimmy intervened.

With her eyes still locked in on Georgia, Mrs. Daniels held up a finger at her son. "Don't interrupt your mother, Jamey. Alls I'm asking is, how is it that little red-headed white boy done changed back to his pasty-white self, yet you haven't after over a month?"

"Ma!"

Ignoring her son's protests, she continued. "As the only visibly colored person that'll be in this, here, house for the next coupla' days, I think I have a right to know."

"Mrs. Daniels, I can assure you-"

"Let me explain." Jimmy interjected, reaching for his wife's hand. "Ma, my wife has had a change of heart and that's the most important thing-"

"Son,-"

"No, let me finish, ma. I let you talk. Now just hear me out and you listen carefully."

Mrs. Daniels face tightened, clearly offended.

"Ma, I'm not sure if you noticed on your way here, but a lot of the locals 'round here find that it takes awhile for the upper body, particularly the neck up, to transform."

"I suspect it has a lot to do with the mindset." Georgia admitted. "You can rest assure that this experience has changed me, but for some of us, the brainwashing and deep-rooted beliefs that I was raised with, takes a while to shift. The reason Rusty was able to change in no time, is because he's still an impressionable child."

"How do I know I can trust a racist lily-white woman such as yerself? Everybody knows Mississippi is number one on the list of the most racist states. I reckon there's more lynchings done happened here than anywhere else in the world put together."

"Ma, if Georgia was looking to harm you, I guarantee her whole body would have turned right back to colored. Happened twice to a detective by the name of Detective Dylan Ford. I'm sure you've heard all about that strange story on the news."

Mr. Daniels joined the trio. "Is it the same fella who went from white to colored, then after having a change of heart and being white again, he all but forgotten about his change of heart and woke up colored again?" Mr. Daniels chuckled.

"That's the one." Jimmy confirmed. "Have a seat, y'all."

"You want me to sit down?" Mrs. Daniels objected. "We've been sittin' fer the last eleven hours." She looked at Georgia. "Why don't you show me 'round this big 'ol house instead?"

"Sure." Georgia smiled, leading her mother-in-law towards the kitchen.

"I still don't trust you." Jimmy heard his mother tell his wife.

"Son," Mr. Daniels said, placing a hand on Jimmy's shoulder. "Remember that time you came home crying with snot-rollin' down your face in the fourth grade?"

"Me?"

Mr. Daniels nodded. "You came home just bawling your little eyes out on account of that Watson kid pickin' on you?"

Jimmy shook his head. "That was Benny Jr., pops. Wasn't me."

"Doesn't matter. Tryin' to make a point here."

"Go on."

"Well you see, son. Racists folks are like little bullies who never matured none. Always thought the Jim Crow Laws and just the awful wrongs that whites in this country done to colored were like school age children pickin' on other kids. It's all just so juvenile, is what it is. Unfortunately, these people pass on their ignorant and bullying tactics to their young."

"Can't say I disagree with you there."

"You know, James, with you being my only child with skin as white as mine, sometimes I feel as if I've failed you in a way."

"What? No, pops. You did a dandy job raising us."

"I said you. I reckon if I had, you wouldn't have been passin' for white and hiding your family from Georgia."

"Pops-"

Mr. Daniels held up a hand. "No, no. I understand. Trust me, as a white man who's business has been burnt to a crisp at least three times on account of me havin' a colored wife and colored children, I understand. Even when we moved to Dayton from 'Bama, life was still hard for your mother and I. I should've prepared you. Also should've taught you how to use your color to help stand up for others. Stand up for what's right."

"Pops, you did. Learned all that by watchin' you. My decisions had nothin' to do with how you and ma raised me. Life is hard for coloreds in America. I just wanted out. Wanted a new start in a new place where no one knew who I really was. That's when I moved to Charleston and met Georgia. By then, I was too afraid to tell 'er the truth. I'm sorry, pops. For everything."

Mr. Daniels patted Jimmy's back. "It's alright. I knew you'd come to your senses sooner or later. Say, whatever happened to that red-headed kid that made national news?"

"Rusty Jr.? Last I heard, he moved to California with his sister and her husband, Seymour. They dropped the double-homicide charges soon as he fully changed back. Julia Haynes gave the thousand-dollar reward to the McGwires, the family that turned him in."

"Well that's good news, I reckon."

Jimmy sighed. "Since that whole fiasco, government officials have been in Saint Molasses tryin' to figure out the whole skin-changin' phenom. They done interviewed me 'bout a dozen times, even after I told 'em I don't know anything. The mayor held a memorial service for all of those folks who lost their lives."

Mr. Daniels shook his head as he finally took a seat on the plastic-covered sofa. "Shame they locked up a lot of innocent folks."

"Yup." Jimmy agreed. "Ended up havin' to release 'em all. Residents made sure to even have the real coloreds who were locked up for petty crimes released. The white folks who had been locked up in there made sure of that. That brought about a lot of changes to the way coloreds are treated in this town."

Mr. Daniels sighed. "Too bad the rest of the country isn't on the same accord."

"Oh, it's gonna happen." Jimmy assured. "Sooner or later, there will be changes. Ongoing changes. Might even have a colored president one day."

Mr. Daniels chuckled. "Sure about that?"

"Got my fingers crossed on that one."

EPILOGUE

"Excuse me, ma'am?" Zora called out to the white woman, who was on her way to the entrance of the Piggly Wiggly's, with a small boy in tow.

The woman glanced at Zora, then at Rosa and Freddie, who were leaning against the brown Plymouth Fury. She grabbed the small boy's hand and turned up her nose, as she quickly walked inside the grocery store.

"Yep, we're in Alabama, alright." Rosa said.

"Hopefield, Alabama, to be exact." Freddie said. "One of the most racist towns in the state."

"Why don't we try lifting up the hood?" Zora suggested. "That way, they'll think we're havin' car trouble."

"Good idea." Freddie said. He lifted the hood, just as the white man they had all been waiting for headed their way.

"You guys havin' some car trouble?" The man asked.

"Yes, sir." Rosa answered. "Do you know where the nearest mechanic is?"

"Must be your lucky day. I'm a mechanic. I'll take a look at it. Let's see here." He replied, walking towards the hood.

Rosa and Zora exchanged glances.

"I don't think I see anything wrong. What's the matter with it?" The man asked, still looking under the hood, with Freddie standing beside him.

"Thought you said he was a farmer." Rosa whispered to Zora.

"That's what his file said." She whispered back. Zora snapped her fingers and the car immediately released smoke.

"Well, that's strange." The man announced, taking a step back. "I think it might be overheated. I reckon you wanna let the engine cool down some. You can follow me to my garage and I can get that fixed right up for ya."

"How much will that run us? We don't have much money." Freddie admitted.

The man looked from Freddie to Zora and Rosa. "Tell ya what. I'm in a pretty good mood on account of my wife, Clara, just having my first-born son this morning. I'll fix it on the house."

"Oh, thank you!" Zora exclaimed.

"Congratulations on the baby." Rosa said.

"Hold up," The man began. "You didn't let me finish. If you end up needing some new parts, you're on your own."

"That's fine." Freddie quickly replied. "Thank you, Mr. Uh-"

"Denver. Denver Shepard."

"Thank you, Mr. Shepard." Said Rosa.

"Not a problem. Just give me a second to run inside the Piggly Wiggly to grab a few items and I'll be right out."

"Hey, there, Mr. Shepard."

They all turned to find a police vehicle beside them. The officer inside tilted his head towards the car. "These niggers giving you any trouble?"

Rosa quickly snapped her fingers, immediately stopping time. "Can you please turn his racist ass into a black man *now*?" She asked Freddie.

"You know we can't." Freddie answered.

She snapped her fingers again, resuming time.

"Everything's just fine, Officer Sugar."

"*Officer Sugar?*" Zora snickered.

Officer Sugar narrowed his eyes. "You three got two minutes to vacate. There's no loitering allowed here."

Mr. Shepard spoke up. "I asked them to meet me here." He lied. "Needed to pay 'em for some work they did on the farm."

Zora looked at Rosa.

"Very well." Officer Sugar replied. "Handle your business and move along. *Quickly*." He said before slowly driving off.

Mr. Shepard turned to Freddie. "Why don't you guys follow me to my farm now? I can come back for the bread and milk after. I reckon Hopefield ain't a place for coloreds to be wandering around. Not everyone's as open-minded as me and my wife. We're not from 'round here."

"Neither are we." Rosa replied, smiling.

ACKNOWLEDGMENTS

I would like to thank and acknowledge first and foremost, the Divine Source, my ancestors, and spirit guides. Secondly, my teenage daughter for putting up with me and my writing schedule. I like to thank my mom for passing down her love of writing and art to me.

The following people I cannot thank enough: My very supportive cousin, Marlene Casimir, for always being in my corner. Romare Hodges, thank you for unknowingly keeping me motivated enough to complete this. Brenda Pierre and Jeremy Dennis, your believing in me from the first book, brought me here.

I wouldn't feel right without also sending out a great big special THANK YOU to my WBAC family for lighting my fire. As well as my second family Sepri, Victoria, & Debbye for always being so supportive. Love you guys!

If you enjoyed Black Out, please check out an excerpt from Negus Vol I & II, also by the author.

The sequel to NEGUS volume one, NEGUS II continues with another compilation of African-American Science Fiction.

· B L A C K · O U T ·

II

Huey

"I hardly get to see my woman and it's not like I can cheat. If I do, she'll catch me by reading my fuckin' thoughts." I complained.

"Hey! Watch ya mouth, boy!" Aunt Gladys shouted from the kitchen.

Kwame smiled. "I understand your concern, man. I really do, but we really need Rosa."

Giving my cousin a skeptical look, I ask, "So you mean to tell me, out of all these people you guys done rescued on Earth, not one of 'em were doctors?"

"Sure we've rescued plenty, but we don't need physicians trying to push prescription medication on the community. Thanks to Rosa and her brother, we've been able to heal everyone holistically. To put it frankly: Rosa's the only doctor I *trust* on Negus."

I clenched my jaw. Having my first cousin as the leader of Negus was supposed to be an advantage for me. So far, since being rescued a year ago, my request for a single-family home had been denied. Instead, I was forced to share a compound with not only my mother and aunt Gladys, but with another family. I had fought tooth and nail for Rosa and Freddie to move in with me.

Usually only married couples and family cohabitated together. Not that it made a difference. I barely got to spend any time with Rosa.

Speaking of the devil. Looking as fine as she is, I thought as Rosa and Freddie waltzed in the living area. She smiled at me, confirming she had read my thoughts.

"Kwame," Rosa greeted.

He looked up from his journal to look at her. "Hey, what's up Rosa?"

"Kwame, Freddie and I are gonna need some help in the lab." She explained.

My cousin looked from Rosa to Freddie. "Okay, who did you have in mind?"

"Well, that's the problem." Freddie said.

"Let me." Rosa instructed Freddie. She turned to Kwame. "I think in order to get a good idea of the abilities of the residents, we're gonna need everyone to decalcify."

"Decalcify?" I repeated, momentarily forgetting that I wasn't a part of this conversation.

"We'll need everyone on a superfood diet. No processed food. Only fruits, veggies, whole grains, and nuts."

Kwame rubbed his hands over his baby locs, then sighed. "This isn't gonna go over well with two thousand residents."

With a look of indifference, Rosa continued. "It isn't fair that my brother and I have the bulk of the weight on us."

"Hold up," I chimed in. "The bulk? I have to go out there every morning with the construction crew to build these houses, schools, and other building every morning. Shit ain't lightweight work. Especially without all of the equipment we had back on Earth."

"Well, Huey," Rosa started with a hand on her hip. "Have you ever thought about how much easier work would be for you if you actually used your abilities? You have the power to levitate and move objects. However, you've allowed it to go stagnant by calcifying your pineal." She faced Kwame. "Think of all the abilities the residents may have that could be stagnant. Freddie and I weren't able to figure out everyone's abilities."

Kwame released another sigh. "Look, I'm all for healthy eating habits. That was originally on our agenda when I found the planet of Negus. However, getting everyone on board will be difficult."

"They'll listen to you." Freddie assured.

"They listen when its convenient to them. This isn't a dictatorship. I can't force anyone to-"

"You know what, Kwame?" Rosa interjected. "You're right. You can't even do anything about the thieves stealing from the community garden."

I raised my brows. "Rosa." I say, stunned. She had never lost her patience with Kwame before.

She pointed an index finger at me. "Don't speak to me. You're not the one working from morning to night every day."

"I thought you two enjoyed what you do." Kwame stated.

161

"I do. I think you two are forgetting that I'm twenty-six and my brother is only nineteen. We wanna have fun and enjoy Negus, too."

"Rosa, I understand, and I'll see what I can do." Kwame assured.

Rosa peered at him. "I'm warning you, if things don't change soon, I'm quitting."

"You can't just quit." I said. "Everyone has to contribute."

She shrugged. "I'll join the gardeners or maybe I can become a meditation instructor, like Zora and Theo."

At the mention of Zora, Freddie smiled.

Continued in NEGUS II: Phenomena

VOLUME I OF THE ORIGINAL NEGUS SERIES

STAGNANT MAJIK

I

"Yo doc! He good to go?"

Some young cat, probably about 10 years younger than I was, with a blue hoodie, Timbs, and a fresh high-top fade was pointing directly at me. Who the fuck was this dude and didn't his peeps ever teach him that it was disrespectful to point? And where in the fuck was I? This was definitely not Sojourner Truth Hospital. This place looked like someone's messy ass attic or basement or some shit.

A fine-ass, thick, Dominican-lookin' chick, with shoulder-length curls, dressed in a tight purple tank top with an amethyst stone dangling around her neck walked over to where I was laying. I became suddenly aware that there were tubes and wires connected to the middle of my forehead.

"How you doin'?" She asked me. *Wow*, shorty was even sexier up close. I couldn't speak, my mouth was too parched and my body felt too weak so I gave her a half smile.

"Hand me that cup over there, Freddie." She instructed, looking at the young dude standing at the foot of the bed, or whatever the fuck this was that I was laying naked on.

Oh shit, I'm naked! The fuck was I doing naked?

With the exception of my large sapphire ring on my right hand, I was as naked as the day I came into existence 29 years ago. I tried to ask the chick to bring me my clothes but couldn't. My mouth was parched and felt as if I hadn't brushed in ages. I tried to use my tongue to conjure up some spit but that shit only made it worse. Yeah, I was most definitely dehydrated and my throat was beginning to itch *bad*.

I lifted my left arm and used my hand to form a letter "C", then moved it towards my mouth in a drinking motion.

"Don't worry, we gotchu, bro. Don't speak." Her large hazel eyes twinkled as she laughed. *Damn, she had some sexy ass eyes.*

Young dude came back with a small shot-glass filled with water. I gave him a *what the fuck?* look. The fuck was I supposed to do with that? I wanted to tell him to

166

go back and just bring me the whole got-damn gallon but I was thirsty as fuck, and at the moment, my mouth was yearning for even a droplet of *any* liquid.

"Remove the monitors from the pineal." The chick instructed and young dude quickly moved to my left and ripped out the cords taped onto the middle of my forehead. *Ouch!* I rubbed my forehead and felt the sticky residue of the adhesive from the tape. I was getting aggravated.

The chick was still carefully holding on to the shot glass wedged between her right thumb and index finger. Now that I was free from the cords, I tried to sit up and reach for the glass but couldn't move. My body was so fuckin weak!

She moved closer to me and spoke slowly. "Huey," *How did she know my name?* "What I'm about to say is going to sound very strange but I want you to try to follow the instructions ok?"

I nodded while I kept my eyes on the shot glass that was now only within an arm's reach. My throat was beginning to feel like it was closing in. *I hope these fools don't let me die.*

"Frederick, don't forget the chart." She reminded the young dude, still standing over to the left of my head. He bent down and swiftly came back up with a clipboard. "Make a note: 29-year-old male in great physical shape. Head full of healthy-looking locs; look to be about 6'2-6'3." Young dude began scribbling away.

I'm 6'4. I thought to myself, annoyed.

"Make that 6'4." She corrected.

"Got it doc."

She began reading my vitals on the monitor that the cords on my forehead had been attached to as the boy took notes.

"Dimethyltryptamine level is on point. Antioxidant levels are even better. GMO have been completely removed. Lead and aluminum are also completely removed, *thank God*. Why did they ever start putting aluminum in deodorant anyway?" She shook her head. "Fluoride have also been completely flushed out. Magnesium levels are back to normal and most importantly, the gluten issue is gone and as a result, just like I thought, the early signs of lupus and heart disease have also vanished. We'll keep him on the protein plants as well as the superfood diet: kale, blueberries, walnuts," she instructed, mentally checking each one off with her finger as she recited each plant-based food, "Strawberries, watercress and...." She tapped her index finger on her chin as she tried to think.

"Chia and quinoa?" The young dude asked, reading notes on the clipboard.

She snapped her fingers. "That's right. I always forget those two."

I sighed in defeat. All that shit she just read and that dumb ass machine couldn't tell that I was about to die from dehydration?

As if she could read my thoughts, the chick finally looked directly at me. "Huey, I know you're thirsty. I'm going to ask you to do something really important for me. As I warned you before, it might sound really crazy but I need you to just try and do it okay?"

Jaws clenched, I stared at her, hoping she could read the frustration in my eyes.

She continued. "So, without getting up or using your arms, I need you to take this cup."

I scrunched up my forehead. *The fuck?*

Maaaan, where was my aunt Gladys? These fools were about to have me laid out on this table dead. I tried to reach for the glass but she swatted my hand away and took a step back. I looked at the young brother with a pleading look in my eyes, begging for mercy. That piece of shit had the nerve to look directly at me and then went to scribbling in his fuckin' clipboard again. I vowed with every fiber of my being to beat his ass if I survived this shit.

The chick snapped her fingers in front of me, steering my attention back to her. "Huey, how bad do you want this?" Her hazel eyes were partially hidden by the clear shot glass as she slowly moved the glass back and forth in front of her face.

This dumb bitch. I was raised to never call a woman out her name but this dumb broad here was playing with my damn life.

II

"Huey, use your mind to take the shot glass. I know it sounds crazy but you can do it. Just try. All you gotta do is try it one time. Just once. I promise I'll have Frederick bring you a whole gallon of fresh cold spring water. Deal?"

My eyes widened. Why the fuck didn't these numbnuts just bring out the whole gallon in the first doggone place? These people had to be from Florida. Everyone knew Floridians were backward ass people. I wanted to get this shit done and over with so I tuned everything out and concentrated my thoughts on that tiny glass. I tried to imagine the glass in my hand.

What the fuck?

Before I knew what was happening, that fucking shot glass was traveling in mid-air towards me! Mid-air! The glass! The fucking shot glass was traveling in mid-air!

My eyes felt like they were about to jump out the sockets and hi-five my eyebrows. I turned to look at the young dude in a panic and heard the cup drop to the ground with a *thud!*

"This is why we use plastic." She chuckled as she bent over to grab the cup.

What in the hell kinda voodoo shit was this? Wait, maybe I had been wrong. Maybe this bitch was Haitian.

"Look, you got one more time to call me a bitch." She threatened with her right eyebrow raised at me and left hand on her hip.

It was at that moment that my heart felt like it was plummeting down a long flight of stairs. This b-, this *chick* could read thoughts! My hope for survival went straight down the fuckin' drain.

III

I didn't know where I was or who these weird people were.

Shorty, can I please get a glass of water? I am thirsty! I pleaded in my thoughts. I was hoping I hadn't gone crazy and perhaps shorty really could read my mind. Shit, maybe I was delirious from a lack of H2o.

To my surprise and her amusement, the Dominican or possibly Haitian chick's contorted lips released a sexy smile, revealing a deep dimple buried in her left cheek. "Nah, don't worry, you're not going crazy." She chuckled.

Where am I? Where's my aunt Gladys? Where am I?

Where was my mama, Grannie and my aunt Gladys? They would never let this go down like this if they knew what was going on. Especially my aunt Gladys. She was my mother's older sister but she'd practically raised me since I was born. She didn't have any kids of her own and we were more like mother and son then aunt and nephew.

"We found you laying on the side of a dirt road in Arizona. Do you remember that?" She asked.

Arizona? I'd never been to Arizona. I was born and raised in Inglewood, California. The last thing I could remember was heading out the house in search of some clean water. Grannie and mama had insisted that I take my pistol with me because....*Oh shit!*

"So it's all coming back to you now, good. Frederick and I were a little worried about you." She stated, walking over with a mini purple flashlight. She lifted my right eyelid and began blinding me with the beaming light. I shook my head from left to right uncooperatively. I wanted answers and I wanted them now.

Where's my mom, aunt, and grandma?

She flicked off the light and those beautiful eyes peered directly into mine. "Huey, I'll answer all of your questions in just a minute, but right now I need you to relax. We're only here to help. I need to make sure that your pineal gland is entirely decalcified before you're released." She tried to reassure me.

"Now let's try this again. Let's reattach the frequency monitors to the pineal gland. Freddie get me another cup, please. This time let's use one of the Styrofoam cups over there on top of the file cabinet."

I let my questions go for now as I felt my body become weaker. My main concern for the moment was getting hydrated. I needed to get well enough to find my family.

"Thank you, Freddie." She grabbed the plastic shot glass from young dude. "Alright, Huey, you ready? Let's try this again." She ordered with the cup sitting patiently on her right palm.

This time, with little effort, the cup immediately lifted off her palm and floated towards me. I lifted my smiling face in anticipation, not wanting the precious water to waste again. As soon as it was within arm's reach I snatched and held the Styrofoam cup up to my cracked lips. I leaned my head back and my throat felt like it was singing songs of praise at the feel of liquid. I had never before felt so happy to taste a swig of water in my entire life!

Freddie, the young dude, startled me when he spoke and grabbed the cup. I had forgotten that he was even there. I wondered if he could also read thoughts. "You should be able to speak now, dawg."

Frederick and the chick both stared at me as I cleared my throat. The way they were both looking at me made me feel like a new born baby about to speak his first words.

"Bring the whole gallon." I managed to whisper.

IV

The chick had made good on her promise. She brought over a whole gallon of cold alkaline water and I think I swallowed it all in one gulp.

Then I went the fuck off.

"Where the fuck is my mother, my grannie and my aunt? Take this shit off me!" I ripped off the fucking cords that were attached to my forehead and flung both legs over the makeshift bed.

I could tell that my sudden change in behavior had alarmed them both but I was enraged. Both the chick and young dude took a step back with their hands up in front of their chest, frightened, as if this were a stick-up.

"Where are my clothes?" I hopped off the bed and my knees buckled unexpectedly beneath me. How long had I been unconscious?

I held onto the bed like a toddler learning to walk as I began to question them. "I asked you a question! Who are you and where the fuck is my family?"

177

The chick spoke up first. She took in a deep breath then released it and took a step towards me.

"My name is Rosa. This is my younger brother Frederick." She pointed at Freddie who was still standing behind her with his hands up in front of him.

"Man, put your damn hands down." I ordered. Instead of complying, he took another step back with his hands still placed in front of him.

I looked at Rosa. "What's up with him and can a brother *please* get his clothes back or do I have to perform more magic tricks? And what the fuck was that all about a few second ago? What did you do to me? How'd I do that with the cup?"

"Frederick, go get Huey his clothes," Rosa ordered with an attitude while looking directly at me.

"And how do you know my name?" I added.

She answered calmly, "You are on the planet Negus. Your government and the elites, the puppet masters who ran the government, abandoned Earth to take residence on a super planet—"

"Oh you mean that planet they just discovered, Super Earth." I interrupted, taking everything she was saying with a grain of salt. The chick sounded crazy!

"I am not *crazy*!" She shouted irritably. She crossed her arms and pursed her full sexy lips.

"Could you please stop doing that?!" I shouted, referring to the lack of privacy I had within my own thoughts.

"You think I can just turn this shit off and on when I want?! Now do you wanna know where your family is or not? I got other shit I need to be doing right now." She snapped.

"I'm sorry, my bad, continue." I urged apologetically. This time I was the one raising both hands in surrender.

She didn't get a chance to continue as I went crashing down onto the hard-carpeted floor. I groaned and slightly lifted up my bottom to rub my tail bone. Rosa rushed over to me and grabbed one of my arms.

"Oh my god, Huey, are you okay? I think you should lay back down before you hurt yourself."

"Too late." I groaned.

She helped me onto the bed just as the boy was walking in. He handed Rosa some unfamiliar overalls and a plaid shirt.

"Those definitely aren't mine. I don't wear plaid and I definitely don't do overalls." I told her before she even thought about handing those hillbilly garbs over to me.

"It's not about what you want, it's all we have right now. We had to get rid of all of your things. With the exception of that sapphire ring you have on, everything else had to be burned. They were highly toxic with lead and fluoride. Most likely from the water used to wash clothes."

"Toxic?

"I'll explain later. Just put these on." She shoved the clothes onto my lap.

"I'm only putting on these overalls. So y'all don't have any boxers or anything for me to put on underneath? Never mind." I said, peeping the look of impatience on her beautiful face.

She looked over at Frederick and he left the room again.

"Now, what were you saying about my family?"

CONTINUED IN NEGUS I

▪ BLACK ▪ OUT ▪

ALSO BY THE AUTHOR:

NEGUS: A COLLECTION OF AFRICAN-AMERICAN SCIENCE FICTION

FED UP: TALES OF REVENGE

BEFORE THE BEGINNING

KOREEN UNFILTERED

KOKO: A NOVEL

PICK ME BLUES

BAIT & SWITCH

DESI EVER AFTER

QUEEN OF MEAN

ALTER EGO

FOURSIGHT

DADDY'S GIRL

BIJOUX

· B L A C K · O U T ·

Made in the USA
Monee, IL
24 November 2020

JAN - - 2021
4/2 0804